These Things Happen

These Things Happen

Richard Kramer

UNBRIDLED BOOKS

This is a work of fiction. The names, characters, places and incidents are either the product of the author's imagination or are used fictitiously, and any resemblance to actual persons living or dead, business establishments, events, or locales is entirely coincidental.

Unbridled Books

First paperback edition, 2014
Unbridled Books trade paperback ISBN 978-1-60953-101-0

Library of Congress Cataloging-in-Publication Data

Kramer, Richard.
These things happen / by Richard Kramer.
p. cm.
ISBN 978-1-60953-089-1
1. Heterosexual parents—Fiction. 2. Gay parents—Fiction. 3. Joint custody of children—Fiction. 4. Families—New York (State)—New York—Fiction. 5. Life change events—Fiction. 6. Domestic fiction. I. Title.
PS3611.R363T47 2012
813'.6—dc23
2012010843

1 3 5 7 9 10 8 6 4 2

Book Design by SH · CV

First Printing

always the beautiful answer,

who asks a more beautiful question

E.E. CUMMINGS

for EMZ

who waited; who knew

These Things Happen

1.

Wesley

A lot can happen in a day, sometimes. Not every day, of course. Most have one event, and that's if you're lucky. Many have less, which seems especially true in our school, which is hard to get into and committed to serving the community but is also, as a rule, unthrilling. Maybe things pick up in eleventh grade, which is when Mr. Frechette, a teacher we like, says our brains have developed to the point where we can grasp irony, accept ambivalence, and acknowledge the death's head that lurks at the edge of all human endeavor. His exact words; I put them in my phone. We'll see, although I trust him. Mr. Frechette can get sour, but he's also pretty wise.

Maybe today's a preview of next year, then, because a lot has happened in it, even without the death's head. School's out. Theo and I are on our way to tae kwon do. Wherever you look, whoever and whatever you see seems glad to be a New Yorker, not just people but buildings, and pigeons, and signs. As for tae kwon do, we've been going since we were seven, and we're sixteen now, or will be. We're both excellent at it, which our *gyosa* Marshall says isn't bragging if you really are and can truly own it. Theo's my best friend, and always has been. He says that's just because he's the only boy in my school who's not named Max or Jake, but that's not it at all (which he knows). It's simple. He bores easily. So do I. But we don't bore each other, and that's since in utero, practically, as our moms met in Lamaze class and got to be friends. He got his name because his mom wrote a book about the loser relatives of famous artists. Theo Van Gogh was Vincent Van Gogh's brother; Mrs. Rosen, Theo's mom, pronounces the name (I quote Theo here) "like she was choking on a *rugelach.*" Theo V.G. knew Vincent was the talented one and worked hard to make sure the world knew it, too. I admire that, and hope I would do the same, if I had a brother who was an insane depressed genius, which I don't. I'm an only child. He died, though, Theo Van Gogh, that is, chained to a wall and crazy due to the effects of syphilis, which was quite popular at the time. I asked Theo if he was worried that something like that might happen to him. "Are you being facetious?" he said. There was a time, not long ago, when we used to ask that after we pretty much said anything; we mostly just liked the word. He said he wasn't scared, especially. His mom just wanted him to sound special. But he saw my point. He always does, as I see his. And his are solid, I feel. I don't know what he thinks of mine, but one can only assume that he finds them solid, as well, because we hang out, text frequently, and dislike the same people.

Now that we're out and free I'd like to get right into the things that changed the day from ordinary to interesting. The first is that Theo was elected president of our grade, swept in on a sea of change, like Obama was, which always made me think of an ocean of dimes and nickels. I was his campaign manager and am proud to say we never went negative, although we could have against his opponent, Shannon Traube, who posted pictures of herself on Facebook giving out cookies her maid had baked to homeless guys, in boxes. Other things happened, too, historic ones, even. But even on a day like this you still need the stuff of an ordinary day, too. Maybe you need it more. So before I get into what took place as recently as lunchtime, we do what we do every day, without fail. We call it Facts. Just simple, like that. Because it's a simple thing, and one we've been doing since we were ten. We each are responsible for one Fact that the other guy wouldn't have known but would be interested in, a fact that has no other purpose than to be a) cool and b) somewhat disturbing. One might guess, and one would be right, that Nazis tend to get overrepresented, not to mention the Japanese (prisoner-of-war camps, not the economic miracle). But you have to work with what's out there. There are certain truths that are universally acknowledged, and you're a moron if you don't know them.

"Fact," I say.

"Awesome," says Theo, which is a word frowned upon in our school, especially by Mr. Frechette. He feels it should only be applied to Balanchine, whatever that is.

"The Nazis made it illegal for Jews to buy flowers."

"Fuck." He stops walking. He has tears in his eyes, and he's not a sentimental person. "That really depresses me."

"Dude," I say, "that's *mankind.*"

"I know. It's still fucked, though."

"I promise: nothing to do with Germany for a week. So what's your Fact?"

"It's French." We both like maps, so I'm sure, pretty much, that he's doing what I am, which is seeing Europe, the map of it, that is, picturing Germany, France touching it, Belgium and Switzerland mixed in there in chunks, as with a Ben and Jerry's flavor.

"France," I say. "Good. France isn't Germany."

"No, Wesley," says Theo, "it's not." He punches my arm. I punch his. "Fact: at Versailles, they used to shit on the stairs."

"You mean the king and everyone?"

"I think it was more friends and family."

"I like that."

"Yeah," he says. "It's good. So now that we've done historic Facts—"

"We need to get into today's."

"My speech."

He means his acceptance speech, given today after he won the election. I helped him write parts of it, the future pledges material, in which he promised universal health care, sustainable snacks in vending machines, and an end to the settlements (our school likes us to pretend that we're real people). Then came the part I didn't help with. Theo put down his notes. He drank some water. Then he said, "I thank you for this mandate. I shall try to lead wisely, but not annoyingly. And now, in the spirit of full disclosure and governmental transparency, I would like to share with you that not only am I your new president but I am also, to be quite frank, a gay guy."

There were a couple gasps, but people seemed okay with it, pretty much, except for Jake Krantz, who has a rage coach, and shouted, "I *never* would have voted for you!" And Shannon had some doubts. "You're sure that wasn't just to get the gay vote?" she asked Theo, when it was over. "You're actually, truly gay?"

"Well, in the interests of clarity," he told her, "you're looking at the gay vote. Me. Which I did get, because I voted for myself. And let me add I did what I did *after* I won, which you might be aware is unusual in politics. I'm just saying. So keep that in mind."

"Oh, I will," she said. "Don't worry." She laughed in a way that I think was meant to sound chilling and sophisticated but wasn't, really. Then she turned to me. "So, are you?"

"Am I what?" I asked.

"Gay," she said. "Bi. Anything."

I didn't know what to say. No one had ever asked me anything like that. I mostly get asked things like have I finished *The Bluest Eye*, or am I really planning to wear *that* shirt, or would I like to go to the Frick on Sunday. But to have a person ask me what I *am*? I dealt with the question as best I could.

"Fuck you," I said, which is more or less where we left it.

"More later," said Shannon, going into a cupcake place.

So now here we are, and all that's behind us.

"I completely want to get into all that," Theo says, "about what I did and what happened. But first I have to ask you some things, if that's cool. They're really important."

I can pretty much guess what his questions might be and, of course, I know what mine are. Why didn't he tell me ahead of time that he was going to come out in his speech today? That's one. Or, for that matter, that he was gay? But enough. He should go first. The big day is really his.

"So," I say, "you want to ask me something."

"It's easy," he says. "What are old gay guys like?"

My guess was right.

"Seeing as how I'm surrounded by them," I say then. "And by old gay guys I take it you refer, obviously, to my dad and George."

My dad's gay, but wasn't always, and George is his partner. George was an actor once, but gave that up and now owns and runs a restaurant in the theater district, in a brownstone. He and my dad own the building, and we live on the top floor. I've been there the past two months, for this school term, so my dad and I can get to know each other as men, since the belief is I might soon become one.

"Like what do they talk about, for example?" Theo asks. "What kind of things come up in gay settings?"

I think of things. It's easy. I'm a magnet, it seems, for a hundred gay paper clips, flying at me and sticking. "There's so much."

"For example?"

"Well," I say, "benefits are a big topic."

"Like in health care, you mean?"

It's nice, for once, to be the Expert Guy on a subject, as we're usually Expert Guy on the same things. "Benefit *concerts*," I say, "to raise money, for various gay *things*. Like marriage, say, or suicide, or trannies. They like to talk about who's going to sit at whose table. George makes a lot of charts. And there's awards dinners, too. They talk about that."

"Awards for what?"

"Their courage, pretty much," I say. "And compassion."

"Is there cash involved?"

"Just plaques, usually. There's these plastic shapes, too, that are like symbolic of something. My dad has dozens." He probably has a hundred, but I don't want to brag. I'm proud of him. He's given his life to the general gay good, and he had a late start.

"Huh," Theo says. "Interesting. What else comes to mind?"

I realize, in this time with my dad and George, that I've been listening pretty closely. "Costa Rica has been big lately," I say.

"What about it?"

"Old gay guys go there. In groups, it seems. They talk about houses, and maids. George keeps a list on the refrigerator. They do that, old gay guys. They make lists on paper. They don't put things in their phones."

Theo grabs hold of this, like a *CSI* guy staring at a carpet fiber. "Costa Rica," he says. "What makes it gay and Nicaragua not? That's rhetorical. I'm interested, but it can wait. So what are some other subjects?"

"Well, there's food, obviously, with George's restaurant. Old or dead actresses. And they talk about Dutch things, like how streets got their names. It seems that to be an old gay guy in New York you have to really love it and know some Dutch facts. George is big on that, anyway."

"I'm more interested in gay things than Dutch ones, though," he says. "Today, anyway. No offense."

"None taken. And marriage is a major thing they talk about, obviously," I say. That's my dad's big cause, or one of them, anyway. He's always on tv talking about it, because not only is he an impressive and persuasive guy, he's articulate and handsome, too, all the things I'm not. When marriage equality passed in New York Governor Cuomo specifically thanked my dad for all his work. The next day, people left flowers for him at the restaurant. One guy knitted him a scarf.

I think of one more thing. "And there's something called Merman."

"Merman? What is that?"

I'm not really sure, but I don't let on, as I like Theo thinking I might know things he doesn't.

"That's more a subject of George's than it is my dad's," I say. "He gets into that a lot with Lenny." Lenny is George's oldest friend. They met at theater camp, when they were eleven. He runs the restaurant with George.

"Lenny the gay guy, you mean," says Theo.

"Well, they're all gay guys," I tell him. "But to varying degrees, which you'll find out about. Same with Merman."

He looks a little worried. "It's probably a sex thing, right?"

"Gross," I say.

"What is?"

"Gay sex. Obviously."

"Like you know so much about it," he says.

"How much do *you* know?" I ask. "Have you even *had* sex? Like where you actually hook up with a real person and *have* it?"

"I really think that's my personal business." He chuckles, with a tinge of sadness that is obviously meant for me.

"So you haven't, then."

"Well," he says, "I did meet this one guy online. We chatted and stuff. He goes to NYU, to Tisch. He wanted to trade pictures? So he sent me one of him, sort of nude, but not showing his junk."

I didn't know any of this, but I try not to seem surprised. "Did you send one? Do you *have* pictures of your junk?"

"Well," he says, "no. I sent a picture of me as Tevye." Last year, at our school, Theo played Tevye in *Fiddler on the Roof.* He was excellent. "I didn't hear back from him."

"But he was the only one?"

He chuckles again, in that sad-for-me style. "Oh, no."

"Anyone from our school?" I try to picture who it might be.

"I must say, Wesley," Theo says, sounding just a little bit English, "that I do think that's private."

"So you've never had sex, then."

"I didn't say that."

"You've done things? Like let guys fuck you in the ass and stuff?"

He looks worried again for a moment, looks down and lowers his voice. "The thing is?" he says. "I'm sort of a top." He sneezes. "I think. I could be wrong, though. I've never actually hooked up. Maybe I never will! I don't know. Who has time? Why would I want to hook up when I could be learning new SAT words or giving back to the community?" Our school is famous for the concept of giving back, which they start beating into our heads in third grade. "We're here," he says.

We are, at Eighty-sixth and Second, right outside tae kwon do. I'm just coming back to it, as I had to take a few weeks off. I broke a toe at 2:00 A.M. at Dad and George's, from a stubbing I endured when I woke up hungry and went in the dark to the kitchen, where there are always eleven cheeses and foreign crackers and cookies made of ground-up nuts. I said, "Fuck!" very quietly, but George heard me and got up. He didn't even say anything; he just made an ice pack and grilled half a sandwich for me in his *panini* press. Then we talked for a while, also very quietly. We didn't want to wake my dad.

I'm fine now, though. "We should get in there," I say to Theo. I see a muffin on the steps, with no owner in sight, sitting there like it's just enjoying the day.

"Wait," he says. "Everything you say seems to be about George, pretty much. What about your dad?"

"What about him?"

"He's an old gay guy, right? So what's *he* like?"

"My dad." I look at the muffin again, and realize I'm starved. "Well, he's got green eyes, like mine, and a similar chin." I touch mine. We have clefts, my dad and I; Ben, my stepdad, says we could both keep change there. "And he's a fine person, of course."

"That I know."

"Like who doesn't." Sometimes I think I could mention my dad to a cop on a horse, or the horse itself, and they'd say, *Oh, yes, I admire him immensely*. "And there's squash," I say. "The game, not the vegetable. He plays at the Yale Club. He might teach me, even, when he's got time."

"Did George go to Yale?"

"He didn't go to any college. He was just in shows."

"I'll have to learn all this stuff, I guess," says Theo. "Not to mention new gay stuff. Maybe your dad would talk to me."

"So can I go now, with what I want to ask you?" I hear the chant that starts tae kwon do, but I don't care. "You can probably guess what it is."

"Why didn't I tell you I was going to do all that today."

"Why didn't you tell me you were going to do that today?" I ask.

"I totally would have," he says. "Definitely. Unquestionably."

"Stop using adverbs." I've picked this up from Mr. Frechette, who is passionate on the subject of their overuse. "Just answer."

"I would have," Theo says again, and more, too, but at just that moment girls pass, the kind of girls I think of as New York girls, although they can be from anywhere. I stop listening to Theo, or hearing, anyway. They're all texting and talking and smiling at their phones, like they were better than boyfriends. The girl with the fastest fingers stops for a moment. She smiles, not at me, I'm sure, but it's a smile in my direction all the same. And suddenly, standing there, I'm *not* there. I know just where I am, though, where I've gone, which is to a park, in my mind, where I lie on clean, warm grass while the fast-fingered girl texts all over me, my whole body and my cock, too, little secrets everywhere. And then I hear Theo again, and come back.

"And I guess the biggest reason I didn't tell you," he says, "is that I didn't know it was going to happen. It came out on its own, one might say. Like it had been waiting, for the right event."

"So have you been gay all along, do you think?"

"Probably," he says. "I don't think it was sudden, like a hive or a nosebleed. I don't think that happens, but there might be recorded cases. There are always recorded cases of things."

"But not yours."

"Well," he says, "this thing happened once." He puts up his hood, steps into the street, looks both ways as if he's shown up early for a gunfight. "If I told you anything, which I'm not saying I'm going to do, it would have to be really private."

"You came out in an assembly!"

"It involves a person you know."

"Really?" I try not to look too eager, but I can't help running through names in my head, like flash cards. Crispin Pomerantz. Micah Kinzer. Jared Zam. I don't know what makes them seem possibly gay. Maybe it's because I don't like them. But Theo's gay, or he is now, and I like him. I'll bring this up with him, but later. "Who?"

"Noah," he says, in a whisper.

We know one Noah. He can't be gay. I don't know why. But he can't. "Are you serious? Really? Noah Duberman? Really? Noah?"

"You sound like Fartemis." Fartemis is Theo's sister, Artemis. She's nine, and enthusiastic. "So forget about it."

"Sorry. I promise I'll be cool. Really."

He looks at me. He's going to trust me. "And when the specific thing took place? You were there."

"I was?"

"It was a day in gym, in eighth grade. Remember how we'd climb ropes and then drop down and do sit-ups, with a person holding down your feet? So I get Noah. And it was the time when—"

I can't help myself. That happens. "When that bird was trapped—"

"Dude? Is this *your* gay inkling thing? Or mine?" He doesn't wait for my answer. "So there he is."

"So it involved rope, and sit-ups?"

"That's the situation. The thing, itself, involved a ball. A testicle."

"Whose?"

"His."

"What happened to it?"

"Well," he says, "it dropped."

"From?"

"His *shorts.*"

"Wow." I wish I had a wise or insightful comment, as I usually (ha) do.

"And do you remember in *Citizen Kane*? At the end, when he's holding the snow globe?"

We had a Masters of Cinema class last year; we saw *Citizen Kane, Wings of Desire, All About My Mother*. "Rosebud. It falls from his hand, in slow motion."

"It was like that." He waits. "Falling gently." He waits a little more. "With some hairs." He shuts his eyes and uses this odd voice, like Dylan Thomas reading *A Child's Christmas in Wales,* which I am forced to listen to each Christmas with my grandma. "And it was *golden.*" His eyes stay shut. His nostrils move. I give him four seconds.

"Golden," I say.

His eyes open. "You heard me."

"The whole ball."

"It's a metaphor, you fucking idiot."

"A metaphor for what? And not to be Literal-Minded Guy?" We have a Hall of Guys, stocked from our observation of humanity in New York. Expert Guy, Lacks Irony Guy, Literal-Minded Guy; these are just a few. "But there's no way you could have thought of the Rosebud thing when the ball fell. *We hadn't seen* Citizen Kane *yet.*"

"Wow. That's astute. I'd say you're ready for Brown." I'm not really clear on what the Holy Grail is, but whatever it is, it's Brown at my school. Brown, Brown, Brown, forced down our throats like broccoli, starting when we're still hitting each other over the head with blocks.

"Was Noah aware of all this?" I ask.

"Fuck. I hope not."

"So you didn't tell him."

"Well, no," he says. "It's not the kind of thing you point out, exactly. He just kept sitting up. And what would I have said?" I can't think of anything, which makes me sad; in all the time I've known Theo, which is all of both of our lives, I've never even had to think. The words were always just there.

"And that told you you were going to be gay?"

"It seems like it might have. Wouldn't you think?"

"I just thought of something."

"What?"

"I have cookies." George puts something in my backpack every day. I dig around and find the bag. "They're called *ciambelline.* They're Italian. They look like fetuses, but they're good." I give one to Theo, who eats it fast.

"Thanks." He takes another. "I like these."

"They're traditionally served with *vin santo*." I learned this from

George. He's taught me a lot. "Which is a sweet dessert wine. Made from Trebbiano grapes, if you're interested."

"And about the ball?"

"I won't tell anyone. I swear."

"That's not what I mean. I mean, have you ever had something like that?"

"A golden ball situation?"

"With a girl."

The texting girl. Minutes ago. I'm grateful. "Yes."

"Who?"

"You wouldn't know her."

A text. It's for Theo. "Shit."

"What?"

"My family. I texted them about it all? So now they all want to meet. At City Bakery, for fair-trade cocoa. My mom, my dad, Fartemis, my grandma. Someone from the *New Yorker*, probably. Maybe I'm a *Talk* piece. My mom says that a lot. *You know what that is? That's a* Talk *piece.*"

"You should probably go," I say.

"Yeah, probably," he says. "Sorry about tae kwon do."

"Whatever."

"I should have told you before."

"You didn't know."

"What other secrets lie in store, right?"

"It is what it is."

He gives me a nickel. We do that when we hear a word or expression that, to quote Mr. Frechette, has led to the "ongoing gang rape of the language of Shakespeare, Milton, and Jennifer Weiner." There's a list, a long one, that we call the Nickel List. *It is what it is* is on it. As are *skill set, farm-to-table, growing the business.*

"Say hey to Fartemis," I say.

"Can I ask you a favor?"

"Sure."

"Several small ones, actually. I hope it's not too much."

"Let's hear them."

"One's about the Innocence Project. I thought your dad might have some views on the subject."

This is a school thing. We stage fake trials for real people who were executed and whose guilt is in question. Theo and I are defending the Rosenbergs (Donatella Gould and Morgan Blatt), who did or didn't give secrets to the Russians.

"I'm sure he does," I say. "He has a lot of views."

"The second favor involves your dad and George. It revolves around gayness."

"Like how to have sex and stuff?"

"No," he says. "About when they knew they were gay. Their golden ball equivalent, one might say."

A new text now, for him. As he checks it I think once more of Texting Girl, her flying fingers, the possible smile at me. Then I think, for some reason, about Blake Lively, when she was young, anyway. And I think about jerking off, just last night, to the jacket photo of one of my mom's authors, a lady who writes short stories about her bittersweet colorful childhood on some island, somewhere, but is also, actually, hot. My mom's this big deal editor. Everyone around me is a big deal something. Except George, of course.

"That was Fartemis," Theo says. "To tell me she always knew. Astute, for nine. So you'll ask your dad and George?"

"Sure."

"And there's one thing more."

"Gay-based."

"Is this getting boring?"

"*Lord Jim* is boring." We had to read it. "So what's the question?"

"Is being gay a choice. Their opinions, of course."

"Have you looked online for any of this?"

"I've been trying something." He tells me this, like a secret. "If there's a thing I want to know, that actually matters to me, I do people."

"Do them?"

"Ask them. I like when someone doesn't know an answer right off, where what they say first is just a start, that can wind up anywhere. Where answers don't end things." He gets a text. It's from Shannon. He shows it to me. *The tenth grade has spoken. Now, let us heal.*

"But what about you? Do you think it's a choice?"

He says some words, to himself. They're new words. "Gayitude. Gayology. Gaydaism." He finishes his fetus cookie. "I don't know yet. I'm sort of tired. It's been a big day."

And there we are, about thirteen inches apart, when he raises his hand and waves at me, as if he is in a cab that is driving away and is about to disappear. I wave back, and soon he *is* gone. I remind myself of the other thing that happened today. "Theo's president," I say, "which makes me Secretary of Everything." I head for the 6 train and decide to shake it up by becoming the Blind Guy, this person I invented. You go as far as you can with your eyes shut tight until you hit someone, at which point you have to say, "Sorry, I'm the Blind Guy." It's more fun than it might sound. So I start, and I don't take more than a couple blind steps when I bump into someone. Someone who knows me, it seems, because they say my name.

"Wesley?"

When I unblind myself I see Shannon Traube, crushed by Theo just hours ago.

"What are you *doing*?" she says. "You looked crazy."

"I had something in my eye," I say. "It was excruciating. In fact, I may need medical attention. So I'd better get home. See ya."

As I turn back for the subway I hear her again. "Wesley? You live *that* way," she says, pointing east. "One thirty East End."

I laugh, not well; it's as big a dud as the laughing I did with Theo just a few minutes ago. "It so happens," I say, "that I have two residences."

"You do?"

"I've been at my dad's for the last like approximate two months."

"Your dad the gay guy."

I look at her while Theo's questions clop-clop in my head, whinnying a little like horses in front of the Plaza; all the answers he's asked me for. *When did you know? Do you think it's a choice?* "Yes. That dad. And he's a big deal, too, in gay circles. If you care."

"Whatever," she says. "I'm tolerant. Even about Theo. People are People, is my motto."

"That sort of sucks as a motto."

She sighs. "I know. I'm working on it. My college coach says I should have one, just in case. In another language, preferably. You want to know a secret?"

"It depends."

"Donatella Gould blew Morgan Blatt. Or *blows* him, actually. It's ongoing."

"Really?" I hear my own voice, piping embarrassingly. Then I lie—"I knew that, of course"—in the deepest voice I have; Chef's voice on *South Park*; that deep.

"Do you blow Theo?"

Somehow I don't mind her asking; maybe because she seems genuinely interested, like she's trying to figure out a thing bigger than blow jobs. "Actually," I say, "I don't."

She sighs again. "I believe you. Don't ask me why."

There's a *ding*; it's a text for Shannon.

"Fuck," she says. "My mom. She texts me all day, with potential SAT words. She says if I don't get a head start I'll wind up at B.U., or Bowdoin, or something. And then she'd have to jump from the roof of our building."

"What's the word?"

"Gnostic. *G-n-o-s-t-i-c.* The *g* is probably silent?"

We pass the word back and forth, like a puppy you're trying to socialize, when something happens that makes no sense. I have a boner, in the street, while trying to define an SAT word with Shannon. How could that be possible?

"I have to go," she says, as if she senses it, as if she's as alarmed by the boner as I am.

"Me, too. Sorry you lost."

"Oh, well," she says, as she walks away, "tell Theo to bring us together."

When I get to Grand Central I remember something George once said, that every person moving through it has one secret they believe they could never tell. I stand there for a moment, right in the middle of it, and wonder: What would my secret be? Is it something you know, or a thing you *discover*, but that's been there all along, waiting? And say you never discover it; what then? I worry about these things. I'll ask George; he's the one who brought it all up in the first place.

I hit the street and walk the few blocks west, and I'm glad I do, for just as I get near the theater district it seems all the lights go on. As I head up Eighth Avenue I hear someone say, "Young man?" and I turn to see, unfortunately, a large clown; he holds out tickets to me, which happens at least nineteen times a block around here. All I want is to get home so I can talk to my dad and George as Theo has asked, but I try to be polite to the clown, as he probably has a family and would prefer to be playing Tom in *The Glass Menagerie* or Tom in *The Grapes of Wrath* (which I happen to be reading in school), parts George says were his favorites in what he calls the Time of the Toms, when he was an actor, long ago.

"What's it for?" I ask, pretending to be interested.

"The circus!" he says, much too loudly. "Bring your kids!"

"I don't have any," I say. "I'm sixteen." And it's at this point, with a typical ticket giver, that I'd take the ticket and move on, but I can see that this guy is falling apart in front of me. He takes off his wig, and red nose, and tells me he went to Juilliard, where he studied commedia dell'arte, whatever that is. He never thought he'd wind up as a clown, handing out tickets to a circus where the animals are abused and the midgets hunch down to seem smaller. To top it off, he's HIV-positive, a condition I learn is rampant in the clown world.

"That sucks," I say.

"Have safe sex," he tells me.

"I do. Or, in the interest of clarity—I hope to."

He asks if I have a minute, and I nod; I'm not sure why. He tells me he saw the Towers fall and that nothing's been the same, really, since. I'm not sure I believe him, but I have a motto that if someone tells you they saw the Towers fall, then they saw the Towers fall, and that's how it is. Period.

"So that's my minute, I guess," he says.

"You can have another."

"No," he says, putting his nose back on. "This is New York, right? We're all so close. You have to breach boundaries and respect them at the same time. Do you know what I mean?"

"I'd like to think about it," I say, "but I think so." This happens all the time in New York, people on the street saying what New York is, like it was a daily tax you paid to earn your right to be here; I hope when the time comes for me to do that, I can come up with something to say. "And thanks for the tickets." He presses a few more into my hand, and then starts following someone else.

So I turn west on Forty-Sixth, and there it is, Ecco, halfway down the block, five steps down from the street and across from one of the boardinghouses where, some people think, John Wilkes Booth planned the assassination of Lincoln. Even though it's early, people are going into the restaurant, which I'm sure pleases George; people haven't been spending in the theater district since the recession started, and he feels this is sad as in times like these a show and some correctly fried calamari is just what people need. As I come in I see Wally at the bar, George talking to Armando in the kitchen, and Lenny, George's best friend, who owns and runs the restaurant with him, setting out pumpkins and maize.

"Hey, kid," he says when he sees me, "how's the meth lab coming?"

Lenny thinks, given my age, that I must yearn for wry and daring comments from adults, so he's got a few stored up for every time I see him. Lenny's gay, of course, but in a different way than George. Actually the issue, for me, is more about funniness than gayness; Lenny says funny stuff so you'll think, "Wow, Lenny's funny," whereas George does because that's where he is at the moment, and you can choose to be with him there or not. He sees me as he comes from the kitchen and waves, heartily, like he's meeting an ocean liner; it's my second big wave in an hour. I wave back and watch as he goes to greet this lady, Mrs. Engler, who comes in just about every day. She's always alone, and always has the osso bucco, which we're pretty well known for as it's always unusually good. And even though she always has it, she still always asks if it's good today and if it's tender. He says, "Yes," then she says, "Well, I'll trust you this once," as if she hadn't a thousand times before. George says people come to a place like Ecco not for the food but because they trust the guy who runs it, that he'll take care of them and understand, even if they don't, what they need.

He gestures for me to join them. I want to get to Theo's questions, of course, but George must want me for a reason. Diner Relations, I'd guess. We have a deal; I make a little money helping in the kitchen—chopping herbs, crisscrossing rosemary sprigs in dishes of oil, torching the tops of crème brulées for that well-known crackly effect—and George lets me in on aspects of the business, like his trust thing; he feels I have a future in food if I want one. I just need to let him know. And I've never actually met Mrs. Engler before; I've only heard the stories. George has lots, and somehow they're mostly good.

"Hey," George says.

And for some reason I start to speak with an English accent. I don't know why; sometimes I think I'm like forty different people, sometimes not quite one. "Hello, George," I say, then, turning to Mrs. Engler, "Madam."

The English thing seems to really turn her on. "Are you visiting us from England, young man?" she asks.

"This is Nigel," George tells her. "He's my nephew. My sister Victoria married a baronet."

George doesn't have a sister Victoria, nor am I his nephew. But that's our secret. "I hail from London," I say. "In England."

"I adore London," Mrs. Engler says. She beams, chuckles, then cocks her head, like Frances, our dead border terrier, would always do whenever you said the word *peanut*. "What was it Dr. Johnson said?" This isn't a real question; there are adults—sadly, often my own mom—who ask questions they know the answer to, usually revolving around a quote from some dead witty English guy or Mark Twain. *"If you're tired of London, you're tired of life."*

"One must agree," I say. *"N'est-ce pas?"*

She is now officially beside herself with joy. "Well, clearly you've lived in France! Now, tell me, Nigel. Have you tried the osso bucco?"

I take it a step further. I'm still English, but now I'm practicing my American accent. "It's *awesome*," I say.

We all laugh, enjoying me. "Well," Mrs. Engler says, "I'll trust you both. Just this once! And while you're here, dear, make sure not to miss the Frick." Her salad comes; she sighs, as people do here when food is set in front of them, and starts to eat. George walks me to the bar, nods to Wally, then nudges me, which is my cue to demonstrate something else he's teaching me, the hand gestures, secret restaurant code. I raise a thumb: ginger ale. Snap my fingers: potato chips. The snap used to mean nuts, but we've had to cut corners; everyone has. Wally sets out my stuff.

"So how was school?" George says.

"Thrilling," I say, "when it wasn't enriching. Donald Rumsfeld came and read to us from *The Red Pony.* And Micah Kinzer saw a black person, and even got pictures, with his phone." I see that Mrs. Engler, probably picturing me walking on some London street, is waving at me; I wave back. "Could I maybe ask you a question?"

"Of course."

"What the fuck is the deal with the Frick?"

"Hey! Excuse me, please?" I'm sort of sorry I said it; I can see he's actually pissed. "Watch your mouth. People eat here. Not many, but there are still some."

"Sorry," I say. "I mean it."

"Not that I have the right to correct you."

"You can. Many do." Which is true; I feel like a spelling test, sometimes, with every word wrong, each part of me circled in red.

"Aren't you home a little early?" George says. He gets a text, says, "Shit," and I do what you do in these situations; I nod to him, and he turns away. *The nod*; Theo has pointed out that nodding, to give permission to "take this call" or "answer this text," is a key compromised modern gesture. And in this four seconds I have to myself I think that George is right; I am home early. Because I'm never not busy; I'm always working, like everyone I know, to seem more amazing and well-rounded and interesting than I actually am, or could ever be. The weird part is: no one's ever actually *said* that to any of us. It's more like it's on all our *devices*, stuffed forever into all of our Clouds; like prune paste in *hamentaschen*, Theo says. So I do tae kwon do, play soccer, coach soccer, and tutor homeless kids; I'm on yearbook, in the Spanish Club, and in the Bob Dylan Society. And now that Theo is president I'm the entire cabinet, and would be Chairman of the Joint Chiefs of Staff if we had a military. And *I enjoy* all this stuff; some of it I even love. What I *don't* love is that I'm not expected to enjoy it; I'm expected to *list* it. Again, no one has *said* that, but it's in the Cloud. So when it's time to talk to guys in ties in New England about why they should let me go to their college, my secret plan is to say what I do extracurricularly is text and masturbate, and see where I get in. Wesleyan, maybe; the rumor is they value authenticity.

George is back now. "Sorry. *Bernadette.*" He whispers the word like it's a code name for a spy.

"Bernadette? Is that good?"

"Wonderful," he says. "Even in the wrong role."

"I don't know what that means."

"You don't need to."

"Anyway, you were right," I say, "about my being home early."

"Everything okay?"

I am often asked that. "Everything's fine."

The door opens. Laughing gay guys come in, with scarves, looking like a photograph of laughing gay guys with scarves. They laugh harder when they see George, and wave to him. I can almost sense him start to *whir*, like one of the Japanese robots Theo's dad collects. George, when he needs to, can be Delightful Guy Robot, or Funny Guy Robot; any kind people need. He's not that way upstairs, though, with us. Up there, he's more just George.

"Hey," he says, "want to eat down here? Armando's got those pork chops you like, with the sage butter—"

"George—"

"—From that green pig farm, where the pig signs a release. And there's *burrata,* and those potatoes you like—"

"Theo won," I say. He looks puzzled. "The election? It was today?"

"He did?" He high-fives me, which I think he thinks I like; I'm waiting for the right time to tell him I find it vaguely annoying and he doesn't do it right, anyway. "Congratulations, Wes!"

"Me? Why?"

"You worked your ass off for him. You don't give yourself credit, you're hard on yourself—"

"Please don't say what you're going to say next, which is that you don't have a right to say that. Which maybe *I* don't have a right to say to *you*. It's just that when you *do* say stuff, it's okay with me, really, because it's never about finding me basically extremely disappointing. "

"Deal," George says.

"But here's the thing," I say. "I need to talk to you guys, about some stuff."

"Is it urgent?"

"Semi-urgent."

"You sure everything's okay? Should I call your mom, or dad—"

George always wants to know if he should call my mom or dad. "No. Really. I told you about the Innocence Project, right? Me and Theo are a defense team, and we got assigned these guys the Rosenbergs. I just wanted to get both your feelings about them. Did they, didn't they, America, hysteria."

"I just hope you don't want me to say smart things. Your dad's the brilliant genius, with opinions. I recite specials."

"You think he's a brilliant genius?" Everyone says this about him, along with remarks on the extent of his humanity. I'm surprised to hear George say it, though. "Does he think that about you?"

He laughs. "Come on. Would you?"

"*You're* so hard on *your*self," I say.

"Hey," he says, "it's a living. Does your dad know about this?"

"I left voice mails, and I texted."

"I'll send dinner up," he says. "So you guys can have privacy." More laughing guys with scarves come in. George laughs, in preparation; that's a trick of his; he says people always like to think you've just heard something funny, and might share it with them. "Pray for me," he says, as he always does, just before he hits the floor.

I stop him, though. "It's not just school I need to talk about."

"Okay."

"And I need you both. If you can."

Lenny passes, his arms full of little pumpkins, looking confused. "Isn't Ruth Gordon dead?"

"Of course she is," George says.

"She's reserved for ten fifteen," says Lenny.

"You're busy," I say to George. "So—"

"Hey," he says, not letting me finish, turning his back to all the waving guys in scarves. "I'm there."

So I climb the stairs, passing 2A, where the Galligan girls live. They never got married and both have osteoporosis, which George says means if they fall they could snap, like chopsticks. For fifty-six years they've been ushers at the Majestic Theatre, around the corner, where they've never missed a show. In 3A is Henry, who writes children's musicals and is into leather. His sister committed suicide, so he's bringing up his niece, Hannah; my dad went to court to make sure it all worked out. And it did, of course; they had my dad. Hannah screams at Henry all the time; she sort of sucks at bonding, apparently.

And then there's us, on the top floor, the fourth. As I let myself in the first thing I see is that the one light that's on shines on a bowl of grapes, the kind that look dusty but are actually as nature intended. I wonder if this is a not-so-subtle reminder that I have a paper due next week on *The Grapes of Wrath,* which seems to obsess everyone in my orbit but me. Mr. Frechette is making us read a term's worth of books that will make us better people, as he feels the bitter, sarcastic irony that he often hears from us is something you should only come to in the autumn of your years, to use his words, when you have earned it from your swim in the harsh sea of life.

I take a grape, the kind I hate; with seeds. As I spit them out the phone rings.

"That's Dad," I tell the air, and I'm right.

"Wesley?"

"Hey, Dad."

"Wesley?" he says again; people are always saying my name again. "I got your voice mail. Is everything all right?"

He asks this every day, like he's waiting for something not to be. My mom's the same, unlike Ben and George, who assume things are good unless you bleed or throw up in front of them.

"Basically."

"'Basically'? What does that—shit, I'm in a bad spot. Hello? Wesley?"

He's sort of shouting now, the way people do in old movies when they're calling long distance. Maybe he thinks shouting makes bad spots good.

"I'm here, Dad."

"So when you say, 'basically,' what do you mean?"

"Well," I say, feeling sort of angry, suddenly, "we're still fighting useless wars, our so-called system is like totally broken, and one in fifty kids in America is homeless." I get like this, sometimes. I can't help it; certain things just *disturb* me. "So, for the sake of argument, one might say, when I say, 'basically,' I mean—"

"Are you getting shit at school?"

I laugh, in a fairly weary way. "Ha! Why would I?"

He doesn't say anything. I don't know if he's in a bad spot again, or thinking. Then I hear him.

"Because of us. Because we're—"

He wants to say *gay*. He says *gay* all the time, when he's talking about a group of people. When it comes to himself, though, he always stops right before the word.

"I'm okay, Dad."

"You're sure? Because George just called. He said you need to talk, to both of us?"

"I do. That is, if you can. Because if you can't—"

"The thing is—"

"So you can't, then," I say. "Which is good, Dad. I don't mean it's good. I mean it's not a problem."

"Oh, God, Wes," he says, "I hate to ask this, but can it wait till morning?"

What can I say here? It can't? I didn't know how amazing my dad was until I've been here with him and George. It even scares me, a little; how does a person become like that? Was he ever like me, schlepping along, as my stepdad says, foolish and disappointing and finding the world that way, too? In the kitchen I see flowers, vegetables, fruits. George goes to Green Markets. Everyone always knows him. People save things, special little somethings, that they think he'll like. And I think: how does a person become like that? How does a person become *anything*?

"Wes? Are you there?"

"It can wait, Dad."

"You're sure?"

I don't know how, exactly, but something tells me his phone will die before I can answer his question. And it does; I'm occasionally psychic, about phones. He calls back right away, and because I'm fucked up I let it ring through to voice mail. I'll listen later, to what I'm sure will be an interesting explanation, like the one last week where a crisis broke out on the gay block at Rikers Island and my dad spent the night defusing it; George said he pictured prisoners taking hostages and demanding to see Elaine Stritch, this old actress who comes to the restaurant a lot. The phone rings one more time, and once more I just let it.

And it's okay, because even though I want to keep my promise to Theo I have plenty of homework to do. This means the only tv I'll watch is the scene in *The Wire* where Jimmy and Bunk check out a crime scene and communicate only through the word *fuck*; I watch this daily, and always feel better afterward. Then I'll go down to the restaurant to see if I can help out, somehow. And in the morning I'll talk to him and my dad, unless, of course, my dad's needed somewhere. It would be amazing—as amazing as my dad is—if he isn't.

"But that's New York," I say out loud, to George's flowers, and cheeses, and butternut squash. "That's New York."

And then someone knocks at our door.

"Who is it, please?"

"No one." It's George.

"You're not no one."

"Me, then."

I open the door. There he is, holding a bread basket covered with a napkin.

"Focaccia," he says. "It's hot."

"Focaccia! Ah!" I try Theo's knowing laugh.

"What's the matter?"

The laugh needs work, I guess. I should practice. What if Brown likes laughing?

"It's personal," I say. "Thanks for the focaccia."

He doesn't go, though. "You reach your dad?"

"Not yet." Why did I just lie?

"You good?"

That's not like George, to forgo a helper verb.

"I okay," I say, also forgoing the helper verb, because I can be an asshole, sometimes, ha. *More* than sometimes. I know who I am; I have warts, and all.

"Just checkin'," he says. With no *g*; unlike him, again. What could that mean? One of my hobbies is close listening; Theo and I both believe in it. How many words are spoken in New York every day, just in Manhattan alone, say? And how many are really *heard*? Seventeen, maybe. On a *good* day.

"Okay," I say.

"I'm here."

"Okay, again."

"Just so you know."

He waves. Everyone's waving at me today, like I was someone actually going somewhere. I wave back, then I turn on Jimmy and Bunk. *Fuck. Fuckity-fuck-fuck-fuck.* The bread is warm, delicious, with little bits of prosciutto baked into it. Which is my favorite. Which George knows.

*

2.

George

This is us, then, at night. Two men, slowly crumbling, minding our business in the bed we flip four times a year to extend its life. I've got my side, Kenny's got his, and from time to time we meet in the middle to do what Men Like That (like us) do in a bed; it's not always hot, not after all this time, but it's reassuring. Mostly, though, we sleep. We like to. We work hard. We need it.

But I can't sleep like I used to, at least lately, that is. Kenny can; he always can; for him there's awake, or asleep; the sheep he counts gather to make him a soft, warm bed. Mine chatter, and dart, and ask for dressing on the side. Have I been in restaurant work too long, maybe? There's that, all the worrying about whether we can keep it going in our little patch of underground Tuscany, and then there's the fact that, tonight, or this morning, technically, something's above us, on the roof. *Greetings, Prophet!* I played Prior, in *Angels*, one of my last acting gigs; those were the Angel's words when she cracked my ceiling and made her descent. So it's either her up there, or it's a fat pigeon, or it's Wesley, and I'll bet on him. Wesley, stepping lightly, sleepless himself, poor kid. Maybe he just needed some air. He's packed in so tightly with us here, in the bowling alley flanking us that dares to call itself a second bedroom. We're used to it, but his being here has showed us how cramped we really are; New York's a place where, sometimes, you're too easily grateful. Now's the time to look, people say. But we won't, because after a lot of time with someone, in familiar rooms, the things you need—more space, a closet, a drip repaired—become conversation, and if you met the need, what would be left to talk about? We live and work here, or I do, like a Chinaman over his laundry, if you can still call them that. And it's not a laundry but a restaurant, for theater folk and theater lovers. "Will you be going to the theater," I ask at endless tables, "in spite of its having become a grotesque, cynical, commercialized shithole?" Or, later in the evening, I ask, "How was the show? Overrated and disappointing?" With these questions I make my living. If you can call that living. And I have to; it's my life.

More steps, shuffles, even; I decide Wesley's doing a sand step, that move of Astaire's in something or other. You fling a handful of sand, dance upon it lightly. Has Wesley even heard of Astaire? Why would he have? Ideas of grace change every year, maybe every day, now. *Swing Time*; that's the one; white telephones, whiter people, black patent-leather floors that never show a scuff. I've got the DVD somewhere, or I used to. I'll look. Maybe he'll like it, as he seems to like most of what I show him. I'd like to see it again, anyway.

And more steps now, faster. I've heard him on the roof many times recently, and have never said anything about it; I try not to ask too many questions. But this is the latest he's been up there, at least as far as I know. Shouldn't he be asleep? Well, no; he should be on the roof, because that's where he is. But why? He came home last night, wanted to talk to us and actually asked to do so. So something must be up. And then Kenny couldn't get home; it was Election Day, which would be his Christmas if he was a store, this talk show and that wanting him to come on and straight-actingly reassure their audience that the Gays will have rights, all right, but don't worry, we're not talking tomorrow (his words, not mine). And as I'm resident equipment charger, I see the four hundred ten messages and e-mails he got yesterday morning alone; I'm surprised his phone doesn't blow up in his hand. He needs a new one. We all need new somethings. Wesley needs shoes, I need the American theater to thrive, so those who attend it will want focaccia and *fegato* after the show and I can make a buck for the first time in too long. Needs, needs, needs. I couldn't sit down with Wesley alone last night; it wouldn't have been right. He needed Kenny.

That's why he's with us. For him. I didn't know how it might be to have him here. I knew him, of course, but I never came along on the Saturdays when Kenny did his divorced-dad routine, and given our depraved lifestyle (quilting, Bingo, weekly Leather-'n'-Scrabble) and the fact that where we lived at the time was so small it wouldn't have been seemly for him to spend the night; it was so small it was hardly seemly for *us* to spend the night, and we lived there. Or maybe that was just an excuse, easy and hard to challenge; I didn't know what to say to boys when I *was* one. But when we moved here, into our theoretical "two-bedroom," so perfect for me in terms of taking the stairs, and not the train, to work, an excuse that we'd never been asked to make died. Lola and Ben came to our Oscar party two years ago. As I was helping Lola into her coat at evening's end, she whispered to me.

"Wesley needs to know his father," she said.

I agreed, forgetting about it until, a year and a half later, she showed up at Ecco for lunch, alone. I was up and down, sitting with her as I was able to. She had an idea; if it was all right with us, and we should tell her right away if it wasn't, she wondered if Wesley might be able to spend the fall semester at our place. The minute it didn't work he could go right back uptown to her and Ben. He'd be with them, on East End Avenue, Fridays, Saturdays, and Sundays, but she felt—again, if it was all right with us—that Wesley at this moment in his life, when he was becoming a man, needed to be with the one who was his father. Just till Christmas. She called Kenny and discussed it with him, too; I don't know what she said but it must have been effective, as when I brought it up Kenny said, "Till Christmas. Four days a week."

I didn't know if I'd like it, and doubted Wesley would like me; even after these couple of months here I still don't know if he does. But I've found it doesn't matter, with a kid, if you know that or not, because from what I can see as to how the Boy mind works, they may not know themselves. What does matter is that you hurtle forward with them, listen without being caught at it, wrap yourself around the endless bumpers they're crashing into and hope you can limit the bruises. After nine minutes with him I'm wasted, pretty much; he may be almost sixteen, but I have some idea of how a parent feels, watching an infant race across the rug to pit bulls and light sockets. I wonder if that's how Kenny feels; we've never discussed it. I should ask him, as in a few weeks Wesley will be gone. As for this minute, what I want to do is shout in his ear *That's your kid up there! Listen!* But I don't do it. I flip the pillow, and slip on a mask, and just as I curl up I hear new sounds, creaks from the door at the top of the stairs, the one that opens to the roof. Then I hear footsteps, careful ones, and he comes into the living room. Kenny sleeps on; I imagine I hear Wesley sigh. He needs, he needs; I've known it for a while now, but what? He said it downstairs, that he needed to talk, but that's had to wait. For a moment, nothing, then I hear him go to the kitchen. Should I bound from bed and, saying nothing, put some pecorino on a plate with a pear, and then scoot back inside?

But I stay where I am; something tells me to listen, no more. I hear him as he tiptoes down the hall to our door, sense his weight shift as he wonders if we're awake and if he can whisper our names. I want to whisper, "Wes? Everything okay?" but I don't, because I shouldn't, and because I know it's not.

Kenny turns, reaches, confident in sleep that he'll find the shape of me. And I'm scared to breathe. *If you breathe, it breaks!* Laura, in *The Glass Menagerie*, referring to the horn of the prized glass unicorn she shows to The Gentleman Caller. I know the whole thing by heart, having been Tom four times. All the notes, all the words.

Another creak, and if a creak can be ambivalent, then this one is. What will he do now? I wonder. Go back to the roof? To his narrow bed? When he came here I finally threw out the thousand ten-year-old head shots I kept in his room and gave Lenny the cache of pre-condom porn, from the time when *unsafe* meant drinking before driving; I kept, mounted on the wall, the wire-work horse head I wore in the tour of *Equus*, for the deaf. But other than that it's his room now, and he's colorized, not so much with stuff as with *Eau de Teen*—hormones, sneakers, secrets, a scent sour and sweet at once. A good housekeeper would set out bowls of baking soda to soak it up. It's too bad we don't have one. We just have me, with my limited English skills. So is that where he's headed?

No. It's the kitchen again, and I know all its sounds; seeds dropping from loaves, cheeses maturing, spoons as they shift in their sleep. I hear him open the fridge and clatter about in it, and I hear him turn on the tv. And even though he keeps the volume thoughtfully low I know the music embarrassingly quickly; embarrassing because you learn, as you march through life gaily, that it's wise to build a muscle to mock your own talents before others do it for you; which they will. The Shame Buzzards, as Lenny and I refer to them, are always circling, hovering, waiting to swoop; the best move to ward them off is to cry out, *Hey! I'm ashamed, already! Don't eat me yet!*

But I know the music and, of course, the movie, too. It's *The Nun's Story*, with Audrey Hepburn, who my close friends know was actually my mother. It's my *Guns of Navarone*, really, a boyhood touchstone. Audrey plays Sister Luke, a nun in a Belgian convent before the war. She gets sent by some Old Character Actress to the Congo, where she assists and falls into hot sub-texty love with Dr. Peter Finch. At the end she leaves her cloister because it's too safe; the world's in big trouble and she knows it's not where she's needed. So at the very end, after Old Character Actress fails to talk her out of it, she steps through a door, with the suitcase she came with years before, off to the next place with no other place yet to go.

Once again I think maybe I'll just pop my head in at the kitchen door to see if Wesley wants me to make him a nice *panino* in the press his mom gave me for Christmas last year; he must need *something*, as he's fifteen and it's 2:42 and he's probably in there growing. So my feet hit the floor, or I think they do, for somehow there's a gap between my *panino* intention and the morning; I wake to the smells of fall—cinnamon and garbage, smoke and rust—and realize Wednesday has happened without even asking me. I realize, too, that I'm alone in bed. Kenny's in the shower, singing some tuneless song, or maybe just talking to himself, rhythmically. *Ya got trouble, my friends.* The song takes me over; I was Harold Hill, at Camp White Way, when I was what? Fifteen; Wesley's age. *Trouble right here in River City* . . . I hit the floor and tiptoe to the door. When I peek into the hallway I see Wesley's door is closed.

"Wes?"

Silence. Then a "Hey, George" from behind the door.

"I just wanted you to know there's juice," I say.

Another silence. "There's always juice, " he says at last.

"There is. And there's a marvelous muffin."

"What makes it marvelous?"

"I can't answer that."

"That's alliteration," he says. "Like it matters. And besides it's not there because I ate it last night, late. Which you totally know because I heard you."

"How could you have? I was just *thinking*."

He opens his door. A fresh zit glows on his forehead, which I work hard not to notice. "Come on, George," he says, on to me.

"Come on, what?"

"Just notice it, and get it out of the way."

I laugh, musically, starting at Tebaldi, ending at Bacall. "Notice what?"

"My pimple." He touches it. "This. It's actually worse if you pretend it's not there when, clearly, it *is*."

"You're right," I say. "I'm nauseous from it."

"And also, could you maybe not call me 'Wes'? Not to be rude, but it makes me feel like a boy in an E. B. White book, or something." He calls out, "*W-e-e-e-e-e-s? You done your chores?* My name sucks."

"You're right. It's a terrible name."

"Really?" he says, flushing with worry.

I see how careful I have to be; he loves his snark, even enjoys being his own target, but the bow and arrows have to be his. And also—I should ask other people with boys—I've noticed that he's not interested in apologies, that it's almost as if he doesn't hear them.

"This guy I dated once?" I say. "He was a classics scholar. And you know what *George* means in ancient Greek?"

"Ummm . . . falafel salesman?"

I don't laugh, as I've noticed that's not the deal with him, not what he wants; he even looks a little disappointed, in me, that is, when I do laugh. "It means *agriculturist. Tiller of soil.* So from now on you can call me Tiller. Or Ag. Up to you."

This gets a laugh out of him, or, even better, what he and Theo do, because they're so cool, instead of laughing. "Ha," he says. Not *haha.* Just *ha,* which means I'm Yorick, Henny Youngman, other people he's never heard of; I asked him once if the lone *ha* meant I was pathetic, but he said it was just the opposite.

And now, suddenly, here's Kenny, glistening, splendid enough at forty-five, with the sweetly puzzled look I find so annoying; either he can't find the unwaxed mint floss or remember the name of a song he has in mind. I always know where things are, he says, and I always know the song. And I do, pretty much.

"Hey, Dad," says Wesley.

"Shit," says Kenny, jumping back. "You scared me!" His towel falls, and for a moment he's naked in our hallway. I know his body; I've conducted a decade's census there, and yet I turn away. Because—and I see this, standing here—since Wesley's been with us we've both become dickless mannequins, straight-acting and straight-seeming and at night afraid to breathe. Would it be different if we had a Classic Six on West End Avenue, with Wesley staying in the maid's room off the kitchen? We were never noisy to begin with, and after ten years together maybe we're never going to be. But now, in the dark, we're completely silent, stone saints atop our own tombs; we don't want Wesley to *hear*—words, moans, anything.

We all stoop at once, bumping our heads like Stooges, to retrieve the towel so Kenny can hide his shame.

Wesley wins, holds the towel out to Kenny. "Sorry, Dad," he says. "I didn't mean to scare you."

Kenny's always a bit stunned, it seems, to find Wesley around the apartment. "I just forgot, I guess. And you know how I am in the morning."

"I don't, actually. How are you?"

Kenny laughs. "George will tell you."

"I've never seen this man before," I say.

"But this morning," says Kenny, pulling the towel a little higher, "I'm right here."

"I can see that, Dad."

"I'm sorry about last night."

He looks to me, but I look away; it's not about me.

"I'm sure you helped, Dad," Wesley says. "The people you were helping, that is."

He looks to me again, and this time I feel a little merciful; we all have to get past this point, dripping Kenny, smelly Wesley, adjectival me. "Trannies," I say. "It was their hoedown night."

Wesley laughs—more than a *ha* this time—and Kenny does, too; I've delighted us all, for the moment, so maybe we're all okay.

"*I* can't say that word," Wesley says, "but George can?"

"George is different," I say, even though I'm George. "There's something . . . delicate about him, something—*strange*."

"And I Googled you on my phone," Wesley tells Kenny. "You were like everywhere."

"And nowhere," says Kenny.

"Anyway," Wesley says, "I'm going to get us all some marvelous muffins, since I ate them all."

"Excuse me?" Kenny says.

"George can explain, Dad. Any special requests?"

I assume a slight accent, shrug, become the Never Satisfied New York Lady; this is a favorite of Wesley's, and he can do it pretty well himself. "For me, just bran," I say. "I need a b.m. before my volunteer work. But I'm not expecting miracles."

Wesley laughs. Kenny looks puzzled. "What are you guys talking about?" he asks.

"I'll explain," I say. "You get dressed." I turn back to Wesley. "And get a few pumpkin ones, for the season. You need money?"

"My treat," he says, and as soon as I hear the front door close I leap at Kenny; I've waited too long for his consciousness, and I know I don't have much time until the crane comes to the window, to drop us all into our days. "Did you hear him?" I ask.

"Who?" he says, which tells me he didn't.

"Wesley," I whisper, as if he were in the hallway, with a glass pressed to our door.

"Hear him when?"

"Last night," I say, looking to the ceiling; his eyes follow mine. "Twenty after 2. Pacing. And circling."

"What was he doing up there?"

"How do I know?"

"He tells you things," Kenny says. He slips into the bathroom, where pictures of me in youthful triumph (Tom in *Glass Menagerie*, Tom in *Grapes of Wrath*, young Tom Edison in a tour of a children's-theater musical) cover every inch of flaking wall.

"Not at twenty after 2, he doesn't," I say.

"Well, he shouldn't be up there then, should he?"

"Of course not," I tell the door. "It's a school night. Or a school middle of the night, in this case."

"And you didn't go get him? Is it even safe?"

He's back, and seems to be looking at me; anyone observing us, invisibly, would think, *He's there.* But I know he's not, that he's steeling himself to make today's Gay Statement. I should let him be, so he can do his good, but I can't, not yet. Because I'm worried for Wesley, last night's Sandman; I worry for boys on roofs. "He wants to talk to us," I say.

"I'm here."

No, you're not, I want to say. But I don't. "He's never asked for that before. Not specifically, anyway."

"I'm *here,*" he says again. "Last night I couldn't be."

"I know that."

"I tried to be."

"I know that, too," I say. "I always know everything."

"Is he in trouble?"

"*I* don't know. Of course!"

"Why?"

"Because all kids are, right?" I say. "Because they're kids."

He laughs. "That's for sure."

I do a few inhuman Fosse moves to allow him to get to the dresser. "It's the Innocence Project thing, for school. He defends people, who were executed, who there were questions about. In mute court."

"Moot."

I Fosse back, to let him pass to the closet, to our tangle of well-kept shoes. "I beg your pardon?"

"I believe you mean *moot*. Not *mute*. But why would you know?"

"Well, because I *did*," I say. "That's why." I didn't; why doesn't that matter? I count on Kenny to know the difference between moot and *mute*, and can't ever let him know that. And he does, anyway, I'm sure, because people always do. Which is their secret; so it never ends. "Anyway? He pretends he's a lawyer, he told me all about it."

"He didn't tell me."

"You *are* one!"

"I know what I am," he says. "So is there anything specifically? I have an insane day, as you can imagine."

"Specifically," I say, "there's the Rosenbergs."

"Milton and Shyla? From the Roundabout?

Milton and Shyla Rosenberg have had the subscription seats next to us for the last five years. Milton never speaks; Shyla is always the one to let us know, as the play ends, how disappointed they are; disappointment, as Lenny says, is its own form of New York power. "The other ones," I say. "From the electric chair."

"But what is there to talk about? They were guilty."

"We don't know that."

"Well, they were guilty of something," he says. "Everyone is. All lawyers know that."

"Would you have defended them?"

"Maybe," says Kenny. "If they were bi-curious. I know my niche."

I see something now. He's funnier, or more than he was, which was not at all. I thought that was hot, when we met, that he wasn't. Everyone I know is funny; I have been drowning in it since theater camp, long ago. And if Kenny's going to be the funny one, who will I be?

"Anyway," I say, "he and Theo are a defense team. So there's that."

"Theo," he says. "Does he have any other friends besides Theo?"

"Of course he does. People like him."

"It's just Theo's the only one he seems to mention, that's all."

"Theo's a good kid," I say, as Kenny slips away again. I join him, in the bathroom, where he's just finished shaving. "Turn to me." He does. "You missed a spot." I point, to his absurdly chiseled hero's chin. Wesley has it, too, which I'd never really noticed until he came here; I wonder if Kenny has, if you see yourself like that, in your own kid. Kenny strokes, searches, but his own missed spot hides from him, as it usually does on your own face. So I find it for him, settle my finger there. Then his meets mine, and for a moment I think we both might forget our waiting days and stay home, in the silk dressing gowns we don't have, to kiss occasionally while watching whole fat seasons of *Friday Night Lights*, to order in sesame noodles in boxes big as cars.

"Dad?"

We both jump, gasp, cartoon cats with tails in sockets.

"Well," Kenny says, in a whisper, "this time I heard him."

"We're right here, Wes," I say.

"I know," I hear him say. "I just wanted you guys to know I was in the kitchen if you were looking for me. Not that there are that many options. Ha."

"Ha?" Kenny says, to me.

"It's this thing they do," I say. "It's the new laughing."

"We're coming," I call to Wesley.

"Awesome!" he calls back.

"Why does he have to say that?" says Kenny. "What's become of hyperbole?"

"*Ah, liaisons . . .*" I sing, suddenly Madame Armfeldt. Which is gay of me, I know, but as long as *I* still know what's gay of me (and I do) I don't really give a shit. I was Henrik, three times, in *A Little Night Music.* Kenny, of course, doesn't get my reference, which is hot.

I'm on my way out when he touches me. "Hold it," he says.

"He's waiting."

"This'll be quick. I promise." He beams, like a boy holding a present behind his back, something he's made for his mom. "You know how I never know the song I'm thinking of and always have to ask you?"

"Well—yes."

"Well, guess what? This time I do!"

"What song is that?" I say. "And about what?"

"The London song." He sings, in the voice of an actor whose rather good singing has been a secret. "*A foggy day, in London town . . .* You know that song?"

"Everyone does."

"It's not about the song, though," he says. "It's about a trip."

"To London town?"

"Just a quickie. More of a long weekend, really. We've never been there together and we've always wanted to go, right? So we pop over for Boxing Day, or Whitsuntide. Anything. What matters is *going.* So how does that sound?"

Can he be serious? Only Maggie Smith can answer this question properly and, since she lives inside me, I have no trouble summoning her up. "Oh, *Kenny,*" I say, all pursed lips and buttressed elbows, "Whitsuntide's in *May.*"

He laughs. "Well, if anyone would know that, it'd be you."

"I'm sorry. But I do." So another small talent I'm embarrassed by, meat thrown to the Shame Buzzards; I know holidays from around the world and the festive foods that go with them, most of which involve almonds.

"So call it Christmas," he says, "because that's when it would be. And no big deal, either. We'd just pop over."

"So popping is free now?"

"It may not be free," he says. "But that's not a problem."

"But it is," I say. "A big one. Especially since my business is fucked, pretty much, and may never get better. Because I'm a step from dipping candles and selling them at farmers markets, in a kooky hat. It's the wrong year—"

"No, the year's right. *You're* wrong. The only thing we have to do is get there!"

"Don't tell me!" I say. "Do I sense the hand of Charles and Margaret?" Charles was Kenny's Yale roommate, Harvard law school roommate, and the first person he came out to (Charles was *wonderful*, of course), while Margaret, whose great-grandfather invented cement, or some such useful thing, heads a pilot program to keep arts in the schools, whether they want them there or not. They breed Affenpinschers, just for friends, devote their Saturdays to delivering nutritious meals to AIDS patients and the elderly, and have every known recording of *Die Frau ohne Schatten*, including the hard-to-find *Louis and Ella Swingin' with Strauss*. I hate them.

"Yes!" Kenny says, as if this were the best part of it. "You've read my mind." He beams, again; he almost never beams. "They've rented a flat in Covent Garden, on Floral Street. Two bedrooms, antiques, actual water pressure—"

"Really?"

"Around the corner from the Opera House."

"Oh, fuck me."

"But I promise you won't have to go."

"Well, if it's a Friday, I can always have *shabbos* with William and Kate."

"Seriously," he says. "We'd have our own cooker, which is what they call stoves there. And one of those plug-in teapots. So we wouldn't have to spend much on food. George?" I turn away; there's a boy in the kitchen, waiting for us, who last night I heard pacing, troubled, above us. "George? So?"

"When would this be, exactly?"

"We'd leave the twenty-third. We've got the miles, or I do, to cover us both. And we'd be home by New Year's Eve." He lets this settle. "Which would be just us. You and me."

"I know what us means."

"Remember last year? How it snowed? And we watched that movie. You know the one. Come on. What's the name of it?" It's Lubitsch, *The Shop Around the Corner*; we've watched it nine years in a row; I don't want to help him. "You know," Kenny says. "The two people, in the store. Who love each other but don't know it. And you made that delicious spaghetti. Remember?"

"Kenny, he's waiting. He's got school; you and I are already fucked for the day, basically. Can we talk about this later?"

"I promised Charles I'd let him know this morning."

"It wouldn't work," I say.

"Why not?"

What no one ever says about clichés is that there's comfort to be found in them; if you know to which cliché group you belong, you almost always know what to do. "Well, for one thing, it was *buccatini.* Not spaghetti. I'm sorry, but it's my life, more or less, the distinctions between pastas. Or among them. Or whatever." And I think: *is* that my life? But I don't say that, because what if it is?

"Dad?" Wesley calls from the kitchen.

"On our way!" I call back.

"George—"

"Don't say my name," I say. "Say his. Because we have him. So that's why, or why not, or whatever."

He knows this, but he's ever the good lawyer, a step ahead. "He can go to Ben and Lola's," Kenny says. "He does live there, after all. And I'm talking about a week."

"They're going to be in Israel on the twenty-third. Three days in Haifa, two in Tel Aviv, four in Jerusalem." I know the schedules of others, often better than my own; who'll be in Belize when, who's having the stitches out Friday, who's taking their theater-mad nephew Jeremy to *Wicked* Wednesday night. "Ben's giving a lecture."

"So that's it, then?"

"We can't just leave him," I say. "He's a kid."

"I know what he is." He sighs. "And we could if you wanted to. I'll tell Charles and Margaret. They'll be disappointed."

"Well, I am, too," I say, and as I do I see why I've loved him, or one reason, anyway; he never thinks of his own disappointment, only the disappointment he's convinced he causes in others. "I'm sure they'll understand, right? I mean, they have kids."

I hear garbage trucks grinding, taxi horns, what sounds like a series of gunshots.

"The bathroom needs painting," says Kenny, as he always does when we run out of other things to say.

"I'll call the guy again," I say, as I always do.

He goes into the bathroom, closes the door. I go to the kitchen, where I find Wesley setting muffins on the *Cats* platter I got, years ago, at a Secret Santa party.

"Hey."

"Where's Dad?"

"He missed a spot. Shaving."

"You mean here?" He touches his chin.

"Exactly."

"I always miss that, too," he says. "When I actually do shave, that is, which isn't that often, which makes me wonder if my future will be, you know, like hirsute. But Dad and me are like the same in that general chin-like area."

Kenny comes in. "Not really," he says.

"I disagree," I say. "Maybe you just don't see it because it's your face."

Kenny ignores this. "Everything okay?" he asks Wesley, and I think: Poor kid, getting asked that every minute, by parents, cabbies, guys selling sunglasses on Seventh Avenue.

"Totally," Wesley says. "I'm thriving, one might say."

"One might say," Kenny echoes, looking a bit puzzled. I'm not, though, as I've gotten used to how Wesley and Theo talk together, sounding one moment like they've just had lunch with Jay-Z, the next as if they were at the Security Council, pondering sanctions. "Well, that's good to hear!" He looks to me. "Right?"

"Definitely."

Kenny's phone rings. Wesley gets it for him, from the counter, reads out who's calling. "Fuck, Dad!" he says. "I mean, sorry, it's the *New York Times*." He whispers this; he's his parents' son. They want Kenny, I'm sure, for his usual eloquence. I've asked him many times to say, "One day, the rights of all, gay, straight, and nonprofessional, will be honored and respected. Until then, come on down to Ecco Ristorante, this week saluting the cuisine of Emilia-Romagna, first ten gnocchi free!" Would it kill him to do that?

Kenny takes the phone from Wesley. "Hello?" he says, turning away and heading for the bedroom.

"It's a rough day for him," I say.

"Oh, I know."

I call out, so the world can hear us, "I can make waffles! They're farm-to-table!" No answer; I just hear stately mutterings from the other end of the hall. I turn to Wesley. "Waffles it is, then. You want to make them?"

"You don't have to, George," he says.

"Then you make them."

"Can I?"

"I'll coach," I tell him. "It's just timing. And *tour de main*. Do you know what that is?"

"What? Tell me."

"It's the touch; the lightness. But it has to be solid, too, and strong." He nods, considers my contradiction. I think, I've never seen that before, or put it that way, certainly. "Does that make sense?"

"Yes," he says. "Do you think I have it?" He stops me from telling him, with a raised hand. "And you can say if you think I don't. Really, I have good self-esteem in most areas, even in areas where I should have *bad* self-esteem. It's my school's philosophy." He never says *school*, just the word, on its own; it's always *my school*, which I'd never point out to him. I wonder if, in his time here, he's noticed anything like that about me, in what ways I'm particular, without my being aware of it; it always takes another person to see that, if they're the kind of another person who sees things. "So do you?"

"I think you might. It's early to tell. But I think so. If it's a thing you want."

"Good to know. Thank you. I value your insight."

I plug in the waffle iron. Wesley and I both hover over it, waiting; it heats quickly.

"Isn't that too hot?" he says.

"That's how you want it. You let it get like that, unplug it for a minute or two, then heat it up again."

"Just a minute?" He's very precise.

"Ninety seconds."

I put out eggs, butter, milk, mix. We prepare the batter together, grooved and notched in our actions even though we've never done this before. I crack the eggs, he pours the milk; I measure out the mix, he stirs it all together. We don't speak; we each just know what to do, and when. I can hear Kenny on the phone, and can imagine what he's saying: *We have to remember how far we've come.* He has become the Big Reminder; I wonder if he knows that. He has an op-ed piece running Sunday, on the absence of gay names in the city's parks, playgrounds, theaters, schools. I wonder if Kenny has shown the piece to Wesley. I don't think so, and I'd know. Because Kenny is modest; he really is. I hope Wesley's been able to see that.

Wesley stirs the batter one more time. "How's that?"

"Perfect."

He pours it in. It bubbles, crisps, starts to decide that what it wants most to be is a waffle. "Like that?"

"You got it. Now just close the cover, and hope for the best."

We wait. We almost don't breathe; he looks to me, and I nod, like the King of Siam to a marching child. He lifts the lid, and there they are, eager and ready for the next step in their brief life. We look at each other, bump fists. Well, he does, effortless as always, and as always I get it wrong. So now it's his turn to show me something.

"It's more like this," he says. We do it again. "Easy. See?"

As our fists connect I see that I've gotten too close to him, so I step back. I call for Kenny. "Hurry!" Nothing, just some low-key buzz of worthiness from the other end of the hall. "Do you think he heard me?" I say to Wesley.

"It's okay, George."

"It's not."

"No," he says, reclaiming the waffles from the iron and setting them out on a plate. "Really. It is."

3.

Kenny

H*urry,* he says. And he's right, I've got to, always, and today's just more of the same. Lunch with Christine Quinn, a trip to the Tombs, the *Times* wants yet another op-ed from me, as do *Slate* and the *Huffington Post,* and I'm so old I still believe the *Times* is the one that matters most. Seven hundred and fifty words on what George always calls *Whither Gayness?* He says I should suggest Havana, for the boys. If I did, would anyone notice? And it is all for the boys, of course, and the girls, and the Bs and Ts and whatever letters will soon push their way onto that list. So I'll craft a statement, as I do again and again; George says I should set up a crafts table for statements alone, with glue gun, pinking shears, boxes of glittering progressive clichés. My sister Alice had pinking shears, I think; she liked to sew, I remember that. What is pinking? I'm sure George knows. He'd pretend he didn't, if I asked, as he doesn't always respect his own knowledge. But he'd know, and he'd say—well, it almost doesn't matter what he'd say. Sometimes I think just being able to say those words—*George says*—is all I need. He's funnier than me, certainly, and I suspect smarter, too; he'd never believe it, but it's true, or true enough. He's always saying he knows me, but I think I know him better; I know what he won't hear about himself.

Today's statements, aside from the boiler-plate postelection ones, are culled from the Internet, of course, our blinkless eye and constant reminder of the blackness of men's hearts. On today's to-do—tackle the online adoption service that forbids qualified same-sex etc. etc. fill in the blank. And there's the Georgia General Assembly, always reliable, keeping up their fight against the employee fired after announcing her transition from male to female. The Last Good War Is the Fight Against Fags (*Don't use that!*). And each skirmish must be responded to without playfulness, irony, humor, so the civilians, as George says, can see that we are, under the skin, just like them, only totally different.

But you press on; you can't turn away. You face the world not as you find it but as it finds you, because it will. *Definitely use that,* I think; it's the sort of statement made by someone who will one day be assassinated. Not that I'd make an interesting target; I'm just the lawyer, the one who chairs the committees, the talking head You'd Never Know was Gay. George wants me to run for something some day; he said he dreams of standing next to me on a victory platform, beaming blankly and addicted to Percocet, a helmet-haired Keeper of Secrets. But what would I run for? And I already spend too much time in Washington, and will be there next week to meet with a roomful of the usual suspects; I'll direct us to the making of promarriage commercials featuring christenings, pillow fights, grandparents at same-sex Thanksgiving tables, passing the cranberry sauce to their sons' husbands and daughters' wives. *Ya know, at the end of the day, isn't it all just about family?* Well, no. Only sometimes. But God help us if we say that.

Face the world.

My face, first, though, hard to find at the moment as the mirror's all steamed. It always is, as we don't have a window in here, only ants and bits of toenail and photos from shows George was in, from that time of his life that was ending when I first met him. He has thousands of stories from then, all funny and good. It seems some people, like George, are just like that, lucky people with stories just circling them like birds, ready to float down for a perch on an outstretched finger. I once asked what his favorite role was; it was Tom in *The Grapes of Wrath*, which he did one summer in the Berkshires, I think, one of his few real leads. Wesley's reading the novel in school, or he's supposed to be, anyway.

What's not up in here are pictures from the play he was in when I first met him. Or first saw him, because that was how it started, with my looking, from an audience, in the dark. It was in some new play festival, some sort of awful Actors for Actors sort of thing, way downtown on a street you've never heard of. And I'd never have gone or even known about it, but my sister Claire had arranged for me to meet a woman whose name was, I think, Diana. She was what I guess you'd call a Young Playwright, and she'd written a trilogy of plays about outsourcing, I think. This was right after Lola left, when she'd met Ben at the hospital and quickly fallen in love with him, and we'd been through our divorce. I wasn't out, so it was before the days of referenda, Rachel Maddow, waxing my nine shoulder hairs. So Diana wanted to see a play, as one friend had written it and another was in it. It was about young women in New York and their terrible dates, and their varied amusing complaints.

And George was in it. He was what all these women in the play had in common, the gay best friend, what he described years later as the Shoulder role. And it wasn't that what he said in the play was especially interesting or funny; I don't even know if he was any good. And maybe it was just that night, how my day had gone and how I'd felt as I'd finally found the place, but there was something about him; the others were acting, and George was just—*there.* I've never thought of a better word (and I've certainly never told him about it). Diana didn't know who he was. "Oh, just some gay guy," I think she said. "You know New York."

And a year or so went by. Then one night, in the winter, I had dinner plans with Charles and Margaret. They were going to the theater and wanted me, as ever, to join them. But I was close to making partner, and working late nights, so I met them after the show on what I always think of as the O. Henry street; you can imagine those stories, in those brownstones; leaves painted on windows, watches, combs. And there was George, in the restaurant. At first I didn't recognize him, and why would I have? He'd been a Shoulder, in a bad play. But I knew him when I saw his hands; he was holding them in the restaurant as he had in the play. One hand in front of him, held low, the other covering it, and both hands opening, blooming, you might say, as he talks to you, as if he might be about to sing. He makes fun of me about this, asks me what if he were the wrong guy; there are hundreds of hands, he says, in New York alone. I say if he is the wrong guy, he's become the right one, over time. And sometimes I wonder what he noticed about me, how he knew me. But, of course, he didn't. I was the one who knew him. I wasn't anything to him. I could have been anyone.

It snowed that night. And in the restaurant there was an old man, beautifully dressed, eating alone a few tables away from us. I watched while George brought him his coat and scarf, helping him as if he were a deposed prince and George an *émigré* subject. He gently led the man to the street and helped him into a cab, and told me later he'd been in the original cast of *Show Boat*, as a boy on the wharf where the *Cotton Blossom* docks. When he came back in he had snow on his shoulders; I remember that because I remember him brushing it off. As he turned to survey the room and see if we all had what we needed, his gaze came to me. And that was it that night, no more than that; I was someone to take care of, that's all, one among many.

I went back, several times, with new gay friends; I'd started to slowly declare myself by then, nodding to men on streets who were starting to nod at me, crafting my first statements, reading my first *Tales of the City* book. One night, after a benefit, I suggested we go to Ecco. I insisted on paying, not because I was so generous but so I could attach my card to the check. *Kenneth E. Bowman, of counsel.* I remember how fast my heart beat as I handed it to George, how he asked us if everything was okay, how Jeffrey said, "Cute," as George walked away, how Jerry, who's dead, looked at me and said, "Are you all right?" I said I was fine, but I wasn't. I was thinking, *Why did I just do* that? *Just to learn his name?* Someone else brought back the receipt for me to sign. My card was gone, and George was, too. I saw him, as we were leaving, bringing out a cake with a candle and singing "Happy Birthday" to someone, some star, he told me later; he'd remember who. She got up, whoever she was, and embraced him, just as we all were leaving.

He called the next day. I was at the office, so when my assistant told me there was a Mr. Seeger on the line I didn't know who that was.

"That's S-e-e-g-e-r," I heard her say; I like names to be spelled right. "From Ecco."

"This Mr. Seeger," I called to her when his message appeared on my screen, "did he leave a first name?"

"No," she said. "He said you'd know what it was regarding."

"I don't," I told her. I don't know why.

"Would you like me to call him?"

"Don't," I said. "We have the number. And if it's important, he'll call back."

I look into the mirror, unsteamed now. They're waiting for me, in the kitchen. "Progress," I tell my face, "will be slow. But steady." My phone rings again. "It's for me!" I call out. But they already know that.

4.

George

His waffles are perfect, and he's cleaned up, too; he's left no trace of last night's midnight raider. Lola says he's a slob at home, hopeless, but he's not one here with us; he is, if anything, neater than I am, which is saying a lot and is helpful in a small space.

"What do you think?" he asks, offering a crisp little waffle corner. "And please don't be blindly supportive."

I spit my little taste into the sink, hoping he'll laugh. But he doesn't; it's hard with kids, I've learned, with this one, anyway, to know when you've crossed the line into the land of Too Far, or to see the line at all. Anything that involves expertise, or technique? *Careful.*

"I'm sorry," I say. "It's completely delicious. Is that withholding enough?"

"Be serious, George. Do you have any meaningful pointers?"

I have to keep myself from laughing; he thinks he's the last word in snark and irony when, in truth, he's the last thing he'd want to be, which is deeply earnest. No wonder he walks the roof at night;

there's a sleeping city to protect! And does he think this is some rite of passage, male to male, the lore of the tender waffle? I just wish I had something of value to give him, how to steal fire from the gods, say, or fix a show in trouble. I didn't know that this was how it would be to have a kid around, to always feel that what you're giving them isn't what they need. "You'll have to wait," I say. "I'll need to talk to the village elders."

Kenny's cell phone rings, from our end of the hall; Wesley and I both hear him answer it. Here he comes to save the day. Again.

"He's just going to take this one." I hope I'm right; I beam that wish down the hallway. "And then I know he's really eager to talk to you."

"Dad's incredible," Wesley says.

"He is."

"I could never be like him."

"It might be too early to tell."

"Not for me," he says, with a little snort. "Trust me: I know myself."

I decide to jump right into it. "You were up on the roof last night," I say. "Pretty late, too." I don't mention the dozen other times I've heard him; I don't want to scare him away.

"Did I wake you guys?"

"I was up, anyway."

"Because if I did—"

"But you didn't." I turn the oven to low, put the waffles on a plate, get them in. "And you made a sandwich. Don't deny it. I sense these things."

He's impressed. "That's amazing. I tried to be really quiet."

"I believe it was tuna, sir!" I cry, evidence gathered, in my role as houseboy to that before-their-time gay couple Henry Higgins and Sherlock Holmes. "And you used that hazelnut *pane rustico*—"

"You're good, George."

I fixate on the sandwich; for some reason I always feel it's my job to fill in people on new elements for old standards, that unexpected something that can make it all seem fresh. "Next time, chop an apple! Fold it in with a little curry powder and a few slivered almonds. I know it sounds crazy."

He doesn't say if he agrees. "And I watched this movie about nuns," he says. I don't tell him that I already know that; I've learned that about kids; never let them know you already know something; let them believe they've brought it to you. "And I guess about lepers, too. And there was this one—nun, I mean, not leper—who goes to Africa to work with this doctor? And she falls in love with him, possibly. But you can't know. You can't be sure. Which was sort of amazing, to see this story that's all about something you can't be sure of. And it made me keep watching, to see what would happen."

"So what does?" I know, of course, but I want to hear what he says; it's like seeing it for the first time.

"I don't think even she knows, really. She just does what's needed. She's *there*, I guess. If that makes any sense."

This is what I've learned he always asks, and always when he's making the *most* sense. "It does," I say. "Is that it?"

"No. I wanted to find out, and it was a really long movie. At the end, she decides where God needs her most is back in the world, doing worldly stuff. I don't mean like going to plays, or buying pocketbooks, or anything. But being *there* again. In the world. Do you know that movie, George?"

"No," I say, obeying my own principle.

Which is where he leaves it. "So Dad didn't hear me," he says. "Because if he did, and I woke him, then he'd be justifiably pissed. Right?"

"Don't worry," I say. "He slept. He's a very good sleeper."

"You did tell him I needed to talk, right?"

I sense I might be in the way. "Maybe you guys should be alone. I'm on my way to the Green Market, anyway. It's the twilight of the chanterelles."

"What are those?"

"Mushrooms. Special ones."

"Why are they special?"

God, this kid asks questions. Recent ones, picked up from the general surrounding yammer: What is arborio rice? What makes something Milanese? What is a Jule Styne overture? I don't remember, when I was his age, asking questions like that. But, of course, I had secrets; my questions couldn't be asked—much less answered—at the Terrace Drive breakfast table. "Well," I say, vamping, "one bite—and you fall in love with the first person you see."

He laughs, but somehow his face suggests he wishes it could be true, that it could be as easy as chanterelles. I don't think he's been in love; I flatter myself I'd be able to tell, but who knows? "Be serious," he says.

"It's true. And it's guaranteed for a year. Less if you meet online."

He takes this in with his usual urgent seriousness; he hasn't yet realized that I'm not worth listening to. "But then the *Observed* Guy," he says, "or Lady, or whatever the case might be, would have to eat the mushroom, too. Right? Simultaneously, more or less. Or it wouldn't be fair, and would be unlikely, one might say."

And now, suddenly, Kenny enters. I was an actor, so people in my life don't come in; they *enter*. "One might say what?"

"You're not on the phone," says Wesley.

"I turned it off!" he says. "The gays, lesbians, bisexuals, and transgendered can, for the next twelve minutes, go fuck themselves." He realizes there is a child in the room. "Whoops. Sorry."

"Like I'm really shocked," Wesley says. "I mean, I live with two gay guys, right?"

Neither of us answers right away. I go first, twisting, leering, becoming Fagin, whom I played at Camp White Way, long ago. "As long as you keep picking pockets, my dear," I say, "you have a place with us." I turn to Kenny. "Right, Nancy?"

"What?" says Kenny.

"Who?" Wesley asks.

"Something smells good," Kenny says.

"Waffles. Wesley made them."

"They suck," Wesley says.

"What's that supposed to mean?" I say.

"What it usually means. They're not good."

"Don't be rude," Kenny tells him.

This, somehow, sets Wesley off. He flushes; he has English skin, like Nigel, my imaginary nephew; every feeling blooms. "I'm not rude!" he says. "It's not rude if it's true, is it? *It's just true*!"

"You haven't even tasted them!" I say.

"Should I wear my blue tie with this shirt?" Kenny says to me.

"Sure. That'd be fine."

"Have you seen it?"

"Did you even look?"

"I just got off the phone with the *Times*, George."

"I keep telling them," I say, "stop calling! We don't want to subscribe. I will get your tie. This one last time."

I start out of the kitchen, but Kenny stops me.

"I'll get it," he says.

"I want to!" says Wesley, and I think of a kid again, one of those small ones in elevators who announce *I wanna do it* when it's time to push the button. He dashes out and is right back, holding the tie out to his dad. But Kenny doesn't take it right away, as he sees Wesley squint at him.

"What?" Kenny asks.

"Blood!"

"Pardon me?"

Wesley takes a step in Kenny's direction. "On your chin, Dad," he says. "You always cut yourself in the same place."

Kenny feels for the cut and the crusting blood, but just misses it. Wesley comes closer, and is about to touch the spot when Kenny turns away. For a moment I lift out of myself and see this happen again in sections, in slow motion, as acts of a tiny play. Then it freezes, as in that kid's game I used to love; early theater, I guess, bodies doing what they're told. I decide it's my job to unfreeze us, so I clap my hands and they turn to me, reanimated.

"Well!" I say, hoping something will come to me. Something does. I nod to Kenny. "Lucky you're not a Romanov, huh?"

"A what?" Wesley asks.

"Russian," I vamp. "The royal family. They were bleeders, or the kid was. They got shot in a basement. One survived. I! Anastasia." I can't resist throwing in a moment of Ingrid Bergman, from the movie, one of my all-time favorites; I'm a sucker for any story that ends on a note of maybe, or maybe not. I cough, as Bergman does. "Grandmama, you are so cruel." I put a napkin on my head, and cough again.

"What?" Wesley says.

Now, I'm hardly the queeniest of queens, and I know you could read that statement as, in the words of my dead friend James from Texas, "self-loathin'." But somehow this kid's being here brings out, from time to time, the Norma Desmond in me, the Dolly Levi, the clamoring Golden Girls of my soul. Maybe it's just the pleasure of referring to something and having someone not know what it is. That's a New York problem; everyone here always knows what you're talking about. They've heard the joke, tried the recipe. It gets exhausting, drowning at the same time you're running in place.

Kenny's cell phone rings.

"I thought you turned it off," I say.

"I'm not totally sure how to do that. Just let it ring."

So we do. But we don't do anything else, either, as each of us knows it will ring again in a moment. Which it does.

"You should get that, Dad."

"That's what they invented voice mail for," says Kenny.

"It's also why they invented hammers," I say. "Because I'm going to smash that thing. Because this place is too small for you, me, and the entire gay and bi-curious population of the whole world, all of whom have your cell number."

The ringing stops, then starts again.

"Really," Kenny says, "it'll go right to—"

Wesley cuts in, which I've never seen him do before; the new zit I swore I didn't notice seems to glow, like a third eye, seeing what's usually kept secret. "Dad?" he says. *"Do what you need to do. Just do it, please, I'm proud of you, Dad. People need you."*

Kenny doesn't say anything; he just obeys, and goes off down the hall. It's not easy, this, being with someone who always, always needs no excuse.

Wesley and I both look down the hallway to where Kenny, pacing, passes in and out of sight with what looks like, from here, a pork chop pressed to his ear. Have we lost him again? We turn to each other, knowing we have to do something.

He steps up. "So, George?" he says. "Could I maybe ask you a question?"

Again, I have to be careful not to laugh; this is how he's posed questions for as long as I can remember, from the time Kenny first brought him to Ecco, years ago. "Sure," I say.

"Have you ever really thought about restaurants?"

"Are you kidding?" I say. "All the time! And this one, especially, and how it's going to survive."

"That's not what I mean, though," he says. "I mean what they really are. Like secretly, in their essence. Would you like me to tell you?"

"Shoot," I say, for maybe the second time in my life. As Wesley circles, getting ready to let me in on what he knows, I take the waffles from the warming oven, cut them into tiny pieces, and dump them into a bowl. He scoops out a handful and knocks them back, like popcorn.

He shrugs, turtles in. "If it's boring, just tell me to stop."

"I will."

"Well," he starts, "Okay. So . . . okay. So . . ." This, too, is what he used to say as a kid, which might have something to do with parents who speak in perfect blocks of text. "So Theo read this article? I forget from where, it doesn't matter, the *New York* something. And it made me think of you."

"Okay," I say. And I feel a little panicked, sense the Shame Buzzards on alert; this happens, sometimes, when I'm turned to people—people who like me!—and find myself facing a sea of smiles. It never happened with audiences, when I was an actor and someone else. But it does in life, like now. "What was it about?"

"Restaurants!" He flushes again, *à l'anglaise.* "Not about good ones or bad ones or ones with rats. But what the *word* means. Literally, that is."

Kenny's phone rings. Wesley turns his head, to the end of the hall and his father, but I want to bring him back; maybe I can give him some of the help he needs. "And that would be?" I say.

He turns back, bangs the table, and smiles. "Soup!"

"You mean like *pasta e fagioli*? *Ribollita*?" My taste buds bloom, dance, sing. "*Pappa el Pomodoro*?"

"What?"

He knows the soups, I know, but he seems thrown. I draw from this another lesson for today, about kids: When they're trying to teach you something, don't cut in until they're done.

"Sorry," I say. "Tell me more."

"The point is," he says, "that there isn't like a specific soup, per se? I would describe it as more along the lines of a *soup concept.*" He pops some waffle bits, to fuel him with the energy to keep sounding more like a lawyer than his father ever does. "That concept being—" He looks to me, as if I actually knew anything other than the birth name of Betty Comden and the date of her death (*Betty Cohen, November 23, 2006*). "Okay, then," he says. "Safe soup." He sits, drums his fingers. "Feel free to ask questions."

But I just echo; I rarely ask. "Safe soup."

"Yes!" he says, powered to his feet again, opening his hands the way Kenny says I do with mine, as if I might be about to sing.

"Because like in the 1700s, in France? These places started to open where a person could order some soup—and please don't list varieties—and feel safe! Okay?"

I am, again, the echo man. "Safe. Okay."

"Because soup back then was perilous," he goes on. "And that's because life was, right?"

I hear Kenny laugh, which Wesley hears, too. Again, we both look down the hall; this time Kenny sees us, lifting a finger that could mean—what?—one second. One hour. One day. I juggle three blood oranges (a skill, on my résumé, along with tap-dancing and risotto-making) and toss them to Wesley, one by one, to bring him back to here, now. "Perilous," I say, to prompt him.

"Right," he says. "And not that it's not perilous now?" We both laugh, we New Yorkers, filling the room with rue, phantom towers climbing and crumbling in the space between us. "But it was different, then. And thinking about all of that—restaurants, and soup, and safety—made me see something." He goes to the window, looks down to the street with its steady westward flow. "Names," he says quietly. "It made me think about the names for things." As he turns back, to look at me, I see his father in his face, the planes in the process of shifting, daily, into a kind of seriousness that always makes me feel, with my show posters and original cast albums, as light as the fuzz a dog tears from the heart of a new toy. "This probably won't make any sense—"

"Great!" I say. "I hate sense, it's overrated."

And off he goes now, with this permission. "A *name*," he says. "A name's just a thing you have to *call* a thing so it *has* a name, right?"

"Right," I say, to keep him going.

"Because you *have* to call it something or it doesn't exist, right?"

I agree again, almost afraid to move, or speak too loudly; the ground we stand on is glass, suddenly. *If you breathe, it breaks.* "I'm with you," I say. "I'm right there."

He shuts his eyes. "Because here's the thing," he says. "Which is that there's really no *perfectly* right name for a thing, right? Because *that* name would have to say *all* there is to say about the—you know—"

I can't hold back; I'm sixteen again, thanks to him, having my first glimpse of the secret wires that work the world. "The particular thing in question. And that's not possible!"

"Wow," he says, slumping over as if he'd just torn through the tape at a finish line. "Totally. And so the thing is, we believe a thing is the thing it is *because its name tells us to believe that.* Like a command, almost, like if it has the name, then that's what it is."

"No questions asked," I say.

"But a name can hide things, too. Which is to say that what a thing *really* is can hide behind its name—"

But he stops himself. I don't know why. "What's wrong?" I say.

"I am," he says. "I'm babbling." He looks down the hall again, to the source of words—*lesbian, Florida, violence*—that float our way as his father moves in and out of earshot.

I call him back. "You're wrong," I say. "*I'm* the babbler around here. *You're* an interesting man."

His jaw drops; I've astonished him. And I didn't intend to. I was just listening. "Are you okay?" I ask.

"I'm fine," he says. "I've just—never been sort of remotely called that before, I don't think. Not like that."

"Called what? Interesting?"

"I don't mean that, although it's not true. I mean a *man*." He laughs and puts up a friendly warning hand. "And like I said before, don't get all blindly supportive. It's not necessary, really."

"Fine," I say. "You bore the crap out of me." I purposely don't say *shit*, just in case, although I'm not sure just in case of *what*.

He laughs again. He can laugh at himself. "You're not the only one," he says.

"Well, screw 'em all, right?" I offer a fist, for bumping, this time with proper placement. Or at least I think it is; as we execute it, Wesley gives me a slightly worried look. "You think interesting thoughts."

"Me? Hardly."

"You do. You make me feel dumb. I like that."

"But you're not dumb!" He flushes; his skin is tracing paper, every feeling evident just beneath it. "And I'm sorry if that came out too enthusiastically, as it might suggest that secretly I think you are, but don't want you to know that I think that. Because I don't. You're not. Which raises like a corollary question? Which is . . ." He flushes some more, and laughs, at himself. "I forgot what it is! But to tie it up? About your dumbness? Not that I actually know anything? You're not. I know that."

This isn't okay with me, for some reason. "Your father went to Yale."

"So?"

"And Harvard Law School."

"Labels," he says. "I'm actually not terribly impressed, quite frankly. Sorry."

"I didn't even go to college. "

"How come?"

"I wanted to be a star," I say, which I've never said before; I see that, and it surprises me. I know I've never said it to Kenny; I'm not sure I said it to myself. When the wish began, I was Wesley's age; I wonder if he has something he wants desperately, and knows he can't say he wants. I hope not.

"So what happened?"

Kenny is at the door, saving me from having to answer. He is on the phone, still, but rolling his eyes, pretending to fall asleep, holding the phone far from his ear. Why? I wonder. These calls matter to him.

"Twenty seconds," he whispers to us.

"So Theo won," I say to Wesley, to get us rolling.

"In a landslide," he says. "Totally demolishing Shannon Traube, by the way."

And Kenny is upon us, demonstrating how he's learned to kill the volume on his phone. "See?" he says. "I learned a new thing. So who's Shannon Traube?"

Wesley shrugs, for some reason guarding his facts, suddenly. "I don't know," he says. "No one."

"No one?" Kenny says. "No one's no one. Is she a hottie?"

"I beg your pardon?" says Wesley, turning to me.

"I didn't say it," I tell him. "Don't look at me."

"Wrong word?" says Kenny.

"Well, yes," Wesley says. "For this decade. And not to mention for Shannon."

"Shannon *Traube*," Kenny says, gagging on the name as if he'd found a bone in it. "God, that's an awful name."

I laugh, not at Shannon's name but at, or with, the memory of Danny, who lived across the hall from Lenny and me when we first came to New York. He has passed, as they say now, which means that he's dead, too.

"What?" Kenny asks.

"Nothing," I say. "You just made me think of Danny."

"The guy with the dogs!" Wesley says. He turns to Kenny, brings him in on it. "He had these dogs, and he always gave them last names. So he'd go like 'Have you met my dog—' . . . What was her name, George?"

"Birgit," I say. "Birgit Effie Melody Fabrikant." I turn to Kenny. "I've told you about her."

"You have?"

"George has awesome stories, Dad," Wesley says.

I want to say, *Of course, they're a little gay.* But I don't.

"I know he does," Kenny says. "And who is this young lady, exactly? Not Birgit Fabrikant. Shannon."

"Shannon?" Wesley snorts. "I just told you. She's no one."

"And I told you that *no* one's no one. If they were, it would be quite a feat." He turns to me. "Right?"

"Her dad's like a violinist, or something," Wesley says. "I think. For the Philharmonic."

"Is he first chair?"

"How would I know?"

"Because these things count."

"Not to me."

"And speaking of stories," Kenny says, "awesome or otherwise, did you finish *The Grapes of Wrath*?"

Wesley picks at the waffle bits while I squeeze blood oranges. "Umm," he says, staring at the floor. "You know. Basically."

"What happens in it?" Kenny asks.

"Well," Wesley says. "You've read it, right?"

Kenny just looks at him.

"So, okay. So what happens is—Tom Joad? Who's the guy? Who

George was when he was in the play of it? Well, he eats the grapes." He looks from me, to Kenny, to me; I give no encouragement. "And then what happens is, he kills the mockingbird." He's home free now, and he knows it. "That he catches in the rye."

There is a pause, which I feel called upon to end. "And then he burns his hand with hot silver," I say.

"What?" Wesley says.

"We should go to more concerts," Kenny says to me. "Speaking of the Philharmonic. Charles and Margaret want to subscribe again, with us as their guests. They say they love to experience great music through your eyes—"

"Because I'm such a moron."

Wesley laughs. I see I'm performing for him a little. And, even though I see it, I can't stop.

"No one said that," says Kenny.

"No one *says* a lot of things."

"You loved that series we had last year!"

"I *pretended* to. It's always the night *Top Chef* is on."

"So record it."

"I hate when people say that," I say, claiming my right to be Teen Boy for a moment, pointing out to the adults their emptiness and hypocrisy. I never got to do that when I *was* a teenaged boy; it could all too easily lead people to the hollowed-out tree where, like Jem and Scout, I kept my box of secret things. "Like it's an *answer* to anything."

"I give up," Kenny says. "And I'm going to get all the papers and see if I got quoted right, for a change. And some muffins—"

I put myself in front of the door. "We have everything," I say. "It's all right here." Kenny, even as I say this, still seems pitched for exit, as if arrested midmovement, turned to stone. And I see something I might not have seen otherwise; he's got a heart, a big one, tuned to creatures in need, as long as they're collected in a mass and represent an idea. Wesley needs Kenny, but as he's only Wesley, and not some initial-bearing group, Kenny has to run. Kenny has to have not shown up, even as he's here. And he can't see it.

And he doesn't have to; I can, and do. I see that he needs to do his good work, unaided by me, out there in the world, and I need to help him do some of that work here, in our kitchen, with this kid who's come here because he needs him more than anyone, and doesn't know it, and could never say it.

"It's okay," says Wesley, who's well trained. "Really."

"It's not," I say. "So you've got us." I give us a little kick-start. "School."

"Is everything okay at school?" Kenny says.

"What do you mean?"

"It's an easy question," Kenny says, looking to me. "Isn't it?"

"Well, no," Wesley says. "Everything's *not* okay, to be quite frank—"

Kenny cuts him off. "Now, I'm going to sound like a lawyer here," he says.

"Don't," I say.

But it's too late. "Words count. Every word we say. So when you say 'to be quite frank,' what you're also saying is that, often, you're not—"

Now I cut Kenny off. "Why isn't it okay, Wes?"

"Well," Wesley says, with the sad-for-us laugh I sometimes think should be his ring tone, "because it's school!"

We all laugh, which feels "nice," which is a word I hate, but hate a little less when it's the right word, as it is now. Then Wesley cuts our laughter short.

"I just have a question," he says.

"Go for it," we both say at once. I hear garbage trucks, gunshots; I hear Henry, downstairs, playing "You Must Meet My Wife," a song from the Sondheim canon which he tells me is especially cherished in the leather community. Other than that, it's as silent as New York is going to get.

Wesley looks from Kenny to me, then back to Kenny. "So," he says, "I was wondering if you think it's a choice."

Kenny looks to me, I look to him; we are tin men now, our necks crying out for oil. "Is what a choice?" Kenny says, creaking back to Wesley.

"You know," says Wesley. "What you are."

Again the two of us, call and response. "What we are."

"You know. Like your general gayness."

I nod, along with Kenny, the two of us dashboard bobble-heads.

" 'General gayness'?" Kenny asks. "Where did that come from?"

"Oh," Wesley says, "you know. Nowhere."

"Nothing's from nowhere," Kenny says.

"You can think about it, if you like," Wesley says. "Because I know it's like a significant query. But the faster the better. I promised Theo."

"Good, good," I say. "I do want to think it through." I'm lying. Think things through? I *say* things; I don't think about them. I see Kenny looking at me, as if he knows this, and feel a need to explain myself. "Because that's a big question. Right? Quite big, actually." My heart races, or at least sprints. *Choice.* I summon my references, from the holes in the wall where they squeak and scamper, with their small sharp teeth. *Hobson's choice*; *Sophie's choice*; *pro choice.* And I wonder, looking down into the hollowed blood orange in my hand: How many choices have I made in life? "It's so big, in fact," I go on, "it should be the *fifth* question, at Passover." I'm not Jewish, but Lenny is. He has a seder every year, where I am always seated next to his Aunt Esther, who brings the *haroset*, which Lenny says, in the case of her recipe, not only symbolizes grout but, actually, *is* grout. "Right, Kenny?"

"I don't know," he says. Then, turning to Wesley: "I'd like to know more."

"That's all there is," Wesley says. "I have this friend who asked me at school, because both you guys are, well, you know."

Kenny and I are synchronized swimmers as we provide Wesley with the adjective, which, at least for me, is still hard to say in a room where there are other people, even gay ones. "Gay."

"Well," he says, "obviously."

"I don't like the sound of this," Kenny says; I can tell his injustice antennae are up; I know him. "You're not leaving anything out, are you?"

"That's it, Dad. The whole megillah."

He's never used a Yiddish word around us before.

"Your little boy's becoming a New Yorker," I say to Kenny. Then, to Wesley: "Not that you're little."

"Theo uses Yiddish words all the time." He turns to me. "Do you know what *mishpucha* means?"

"But your *question*," Kenny says. "Is someone giving you shit?"

"No," he says. "There's no shit involved here, Dad, okay? Just believe me."

"None? You're sure?"

"Dad?" says Wesley. "Not to be offensive or anything? But you guys are boring, in a way."

Kenny and I look at each other. "Who wants cocoa?" I say. "We're boring."

"There's this one boy?" Wesley goes on. "Morgan Blatt? *His* dad was like a lawyer, then he became a woman and decided he hated being a lawyer. Now he's doing nails. And this other boy, Max Bloom? He lives with his mom, and his mom's girlfriend, and his mom's girlfriend's girlfriend."

Kenny and I are, again, a double act. "Really!"

"Right. I think she got out of Cuba on a boat filled with lesbians. The girlfriend's girlfriend, that is. So, have you guys seen my backpack? I don't want to forget, there's something you're supposed to sign."

"George has," Kenny says, without thinking; as I know him, he knows me.

"Hall closet," I say.

"Awesome," Wesley says, grabbing a muffin.

As soon as he's out, Kenny turns to me and whispers, "Have you noticed? Since he's been here, he seems to put everything in the form of a question?"

"They all do that," I hiss back.

"I never did," he says. "Should we ask Lola to say something?"

Wesley is back with us now, holding out a paper for Kenny to sign. Kenny turns to me, which means *Have you seen my glasses?* I have, for I have taken to carrying an extra pair of his in my pocket at all times. I don't mind; I like solving problems that can actually be solved. And so, in our gavotte, I bow and hand him what he needs.

"What is this?" Kenny asks, ever the lawyer, suspicious of things that need signatures.

"It's nothing," Wesley says. "It's just permission for the ski trip." He turns to me, as if I'd just said, *But you know we can't afford that, dear.* "And it's only a weekend, and I've got the money saved up from working downstairs, thanks to George." Kenny is studying it as if it were the Warren Commission Report. "And me and Theo are sharing a room, which makes it even less—"

Kenny puts down the consent slip, hands his glasses back to me. "About your question."

"Yes?"

"I don't think I'll need to think about it," Kenny says.

"You don't?" Wesley asks.

"No," he says.

If you breathe.

"So what you're saying, Dad, is—"

"*No.* I'm saying that's my answer."

"You don't think it's a choice—"

Everything seems to wait; some sounds and smells come in, like company, through the door Wesley has left open, while Kenny considers what he's going to say. I smell garlic, five hundred cloves' worth, sautéed by Armando until the edges are golden, and I hear Henry, on to *Passion* in his Steve Loop, singing "I Read," complete with the prelude of Fosca's offstage scream. "Dad?" Wesley says.

Kenny looks to me, though, not to him. He hasn't lost anything that he needs me to find; I know all those looks. This look is different, and somehow I feel it says, *Listen well.*

"No, I don't," he says.

"Would you mind if I wrote something down?"

"Why would you want to do that?"

"Because what you say is always interesting to me, frankly."

Kenny seems surprised. "It is?"

"Yes! So I want to make sure I get it right."

He takes a pen and legal pad from his backpack and writes the word *DAD*, in chunky red letters, earnestly showing a tip of tongue.

"So, okay," he says "You, Dad, personally believe that being gay is not a choice, because—"

Kenny sits up straight, which is always a sign that he knows exactly what he is going to say. "Because," he says, "why would anyone actually *choose* a way of life that they know will make life harder." He's set this out, as a truth held to be self-evident; no question mark was needed because the question, if it was ever open, is now closed. He turns to me, all the same, even though he knows what I'm going to say because there's nothing *to* say. "Right, George?"

They're both looking at me; I know I should just echo what Kenny said, and what everyone says, because it's right, it's clearly the right thing to say. But I go dry. "Could I think about that?"

"Sure," says Wesley. "But if you could let me know by tonight, it would be great, because like I said, it's semiurgent."

Kenny looks at his watch. "And I have to get going," he says.

"I just have one more question, Dad."

Kenny turns to me. "Could you take this one, possibly?"

But Wesley's right there, hanging in; I'm impressed, really. "So how did you know?"

We team up again, Kenny and I. "Know?"

"How did you know that you were gay?" Wesley says. "That your life would have gayness in it."

I go blank, even though this is the question asked of every gay man on every first date, by every new gay friend, by cashiers at Trader Joe's. *When did you know?* No one ever asks, though, *Are you sure?*

"Is this for a class?" Kenny asks.

"In a way," he says.

"Just in a way?" says Kenny.

"It's more for a friend."

"What kind of friend?"

"Well, a gay one, obviously," Wesley says.

Kenny looks to me.

"Could I think about that one, too?" I say.

"Sure," Wesley says. "What about you, Dad?"

"This we can talk about later—"

"But we won't. We never talk about things."

"We talk about plenty of things!"

"The gay this, gay that. Task forces, statues, the *Joads*—"

I can't help myself; I was an actor for a long time, and of all my Toms, Tom Joad was my favorite. It's been years; do I still have the words? I open with a sound effect.

"What are you doing?" says Kenny.

"It's a train whistle," I say. "Moving through the Dust Bowl at 2 in the morning."

"Why are you doing that?"

"I'll be there, Ma," I say.

" 'Ma'?" says Kenny.

"Where will you be?" Wesley asks.

Once you play a part, it never fully leaves you; it just waits for a chance to come back. *"Wherever you look I'll be there . . . and when folks eat the stuff they raise . . . why, I'll be there, too. . . ."*

Father and son are now a team, sharing a blank stare.

"The movie," I say. "*Grapes of Wrath*."

"It's a movie?" Wesley says. "Not just a book?"

"Both. It got lucky. That was my Henry Fonda impression, by the way. He played Tom."

"Who?"

"Jane's father."

"Who?"

Again, and again; he doesn't know anything. They, the Young, have every fact that ever was or will be an inch from their face on a glowing screen, and none of them know Ginger Rogers from Mary, Queen of Scots, or seem, particularly, to want to. He's not like I was at his age, which makes sense; he's not me. But I knew everything, always, because I wanted to, and I had to as well. I sensed I'd need to *refer* to this, that, that it was a way of saying, *I'm like you*. Having Wesley here? He makes me see things about myself I've never seen, and has no idea he's doing it. And some of them I don't like.

"Ignore me," I say. "I'm not here. Even though I just said I would be. But that was Tom talking."

Kenny takes over before I start to load the truck with our few possessions for the dusty drive west. "Okay," he says, "you wanted to know how I knew I was gay."

Wesley pulls out the phone, to get ready, the Hildy Johnson bitten pencil and pocket pad one more thing that's gone forever. "That'd be awesome—" he says, then quickly corrects himself. "Even though I'm not supposed to use that word. Well, that's what Mom says."

"Why does she say that?" George asks.

"Because it makes me seem ordinary. And I'm so totally clearly not. Ha." He breathes on his phone, buffs it with his hoodie. "So—"

"Tell me one thing," says Kenny. "Why do you want to know? You've never shown interest before."

"I've never been with you long enough."

"That's bullshit, Wesley."

"Saturdays," he says. "And like I'm *really* going to say in the Arms and Armor Hall or the Apple Store, 'So, Dad, would you please plow the furrows of your gayness for me and then could we maybe have Thai food?"

"You're actually interested?" Kenny says.

"Extremely."

Kenny turns into a lawyer, which he often does, despite the fact that he already is one. "I'll need to know why. You say this is for a friend."

"For Theo," says Wesley, "in the interest of clarity."

"Theo," Kenny says, turning to me as if to say, "See?"

"Theo," I say, to make it a magic three. And what I recall now, which I keep to myself, is that he came on his own into Ecco last week. He had a backpack and a book, and ordered spaghetti with butter, no cheese. I didn't see him right away as I was in the kitchen, but when I did I asked if he was meeting Wesley and he told me no, he wasn't, but if I had a second could he ask me a question? I said sure, which was when three huge parties showed up, and I had to go be *George! The Musical*, an eleven o'clock number, disguised as a man. When I got back Theo was gone, leaving behind an empty bowl and a twenty, having asked Lenny to tell me he wanted to know how I felt about my life, and it would be fine with him if I wanted to submit my answer by e-mail, or even text if I knew how to do it. I forgot to tell Wesley; so many things happen each night, I'm the audience for a thousand little plays. Or maybe something told me to wait. I'd like to think it was that, but then I'd like to think a lot of things. And I haven't gotten around to it, which might be because I don't know what my answer would be.

"Remember how Theo was running for tenth grade president?" Wesley says.

"And he won!" I say, a little too brightly, maybe.

"Would you mind letting me tell it, George?"

"Don't be rude," says Kenny.

"He wasn't," I say. "He's right."

"So he made this acceptance speech," Wesley says, "which was really good, maybe a little long. But it had an unusual ending."

"Yes?" I say. The kid can tell a story. He really can.

"He came out."

"Excuse me?" Kenny says.

"Theo came out. As a gay person."

"Did he?" Kenny and I say, in our new close harmony.

"*Ex tempore.*"

"What?" I say.

"Latin," Wesley says. He loves Latin. I think he won a prize for it. "Sort of like *offhand.* Right, Dad?"

Kenny loves Latin, too. Wesley told me, when I asked why he was taking it, that it was because of him. "Yes," Kenny says. "Basically."

"And he won!" I say again, as if I wanted to make sure it was still true. "I think it's great. Sometimes I wish I was gay today. Even though I am gay today. But young." They look at me. "Instead of old. Hopeful! But the big thing is—" A few tears come, and as I don't want Wesley to see them I turn to scrub a patch of counter that doesn't need scrubbing. When I turn back I say, "Right, Kenny?" and as I do it occurs to me that since Wesley's been here not only are we silent on our side of the wall, we're formal and guiltless in how we address each other, too: He is "Kenny," I am "George," as if we'd met at an intermission, introduced by a mutual friend, found each other attractive but not quite attractive enough to do anything about it. Never "honey," or "sweetheart," which doesn't mean I think we should do it in Wesley's presence. But we don't do it in private, either.

"And Shannon lost," Wesley says. "Traube. With the awful

name." He's beaming now, having gotten what he wanted, nuggets for his friend and the promise of more for later. "So thanks, you guys. From both of us. And so the transition begins."

"Of what?" Kenny says.

"The tenth grade government. See you!"

And that's it. He's gone.

We each take a breath. We look at each other, feeling the need to say something and hoping the other one goes first. This turns out to be moot, or mute, or whatever the right word is, because Wesley has tiptoed back, smiling even as he scares the shit out of us.

"After all that," he says, "I forgot my *Grapes of Wrath*!" He scoops it up and is on his way out again when I remember what I promised his mom.

"You need shoes," I call out after him.

"I have shoes!"

"Those aren't shoes."

"George—"

"Your mother hates them," I say, going out into the hall.

"So?"

"Your grandma's birthday is in two weeks, and she begged me to help. I told her I'd take you. So I will. And you'll like it."

"Ha," he says, going out and shutting the door behind him.

"Interesting," Kenny says when I come back.

"Theo?"

"The questions, I mean. Just out of the blue like that."

"But how blue is it, though?"

"What do you mean?" asks Kenny.

"He's been with us," I say. "He sees, he hears. He's not like some apple, in a bowl. He's interested in you, Kenny. He wants to know you. That's why he's here. So there's no blue. Not really. And nothing's coming out of it."

He looks at his phone. "I have twenty-two messages, in the last four minutes."

"Well," I say, "you'd better start chipping away. People need you."

"Really?" he says.

"Go," I say.

So he does, and I know I need to as well, to support local farmers who if they were any good wouldn't be local. I wouldn't mind a final moment with Kenny before we're shot into our days, but I hear him, down the hall, making a *Whither Gayness* statement and I don't want to interrupt that. I get my keys, collapse my shopping cart, and see that Wesley has left the *Times* on a chair. Part of his homework is to read three editorials (blogs don't count) before school each day; as I try to make sense of his yellow Hi-Lites I remember something I haven't thought of in years. I was on a train, with my dad; he taught me how to fold the paper into an oblong so as not to intrude on the space of other passengers. "If you can fold a paper on a moving train," he said, "you're more or less set for life." Well, I'm set, I guess, for something, as I'm still able to do it. I could show Wesley, I suppose, but what good would it do him? By the time he's ready to fold the *Times* on trains papers will be dead, it seems, replaced by bits of text on screens light as a Coward play and small as a stamp. And there'll be some new trick that will make you set for life, for fathers to teach sons.

But that's for Kenny, to figure that out. What I can do for Wesley is tuck *ciambelline* into his backpack and take him to buy shoes, so Lola can live without shame and he can go back, properly shod, to

East End Avenue after his wilderness adventure in the theater district. And we'll be here, with our corn pads and our Netflix queue, as we were before he came and will be when he's gone, taking care of people, theatergoers for me, suffering gay masses for Kenny, two groups that intersect with surprising ease. "*Caution,*" I hear Kenny say. "*Careful.*" If a fag landed on the moon, he wouldn't take a giant leap for mankind. He'd take baby steps, silent ones, so as not to startle any little green men.

So I tiptoe out, with my Green Market wad of singles and Basque farm wife's bonnet. There's this hippy there, smelly but nice, who every few weeks descends from New Paltz with three perfect goat cheeses; if I hurry I might be able to bring one home and use it in something tonight. A salad, maybe? A pizza? Crumbled into *bucatini* with a few chopped herbs? I'll think of something, by tonight. Something delicious. Because it's my job, and because I love it, and because I always do.

5.

Theo

I didn't plan it; in a way, it seems, it planned *me.* I won, and I was making my acceptance speech, and then the words were there, all excited, like kids going off to camp. *I. Am. Gay.* It might have been part of a phenomenon that Wesley and I have noticed sometimes, which is how you think *you're* living your life, but your life has ideas of its own. I should point out that I don't actually remember what I said up there, but Wesley will, for my biographers (ha). He remembers most smart or funny things a person says. I do, too. But it's different, with yourself. It just is. You need the other person.

When I met my mom, dad, Fartemis, and grandma at City I was sort of forced to relive the whole day: winning, the speech, my own surprise at what came out of me.

"It breaks my heart to think of the *torment* you must have undergone," my mom said.

"Can I get a different marshmallow?" Fartemis asked. We were all having cocoa, which is excellent there. "This one's like all *hard.*"

"It wasn't that bad," I said.

"The marshmallow?" said Fartemis.

"The torment. Or may be it was, and I didn't know it."

My mom gave her some money, She went to the counter, skipping.

"So you didn't know?" my dad said. "That's possible?"

"No, I knew," I said. "But in the way you like know a person you've met a few times, over a few years, say. I knew the *face,* of the gayness. Just not well. But I'd be lying if I said gayness and I had never actually met, to round out my metaphor."

For what seemed like a long time no one said anything. We sipped cocoa. Fartemis came back, and tore off half of her new marshmallow to give to me.

Then my mom said, sort of sadly, "So there wasn't that much torment?"

"It's a new world, Betsy," my grandma said. "Get with it! Right, darling?"

"Right, Grandma," I said.

"Well, this is quite a day," said my mom. "I think we—"

"I'm gay, too, you know," Fartemis said.

My mom looked to my dad. "I doubt that, sweetheart," she said. "And if you were, which you're not, Daddy and I would embrace it, and you."

"I love lesbians," my grandma said. "They've always found me attractive. I could tell you stories!"

My dad nudged me with his foot, under the table. He likes to do that, and mutter things. "It can be hot," he muttered. "Though not with her."

"I want a wife," Fartemis said. "Ms. Penni has a wife." Ms. Penni is one of her teachers. "Her name is Mike. She came to our class and showed us how to install alarm systems."

Then my grandma took my hand again. She had ketchup on her

dress, which I tried not to stare at, as she's been widowed, twice. "And I say, bravo! In fact," she said, looking to my mom, "I told Ted Goulée about it. And don't make that face. Ted's *much* more a friend than a decorator. He and Javier want Theo to come to lunch. At their *apartment*."

My grandma and mom sort of had a fight. It was like I wasn't there, in a way. I texted Wesley: *Help*.

"Mother," my mom said, "it *is* a new world, to quote you. And Ted is seventy. Somehow I don't see Theo schlepping around the Upper East Side with a bag of gimp and fabric swatches."

"What's gimp?" Fartemis asked.

"It's what can *make* a room," said my grandma.

Then my dad stepped in. He's good at that, and on my side, always. If I'm gay, which I am, it's not because my dad was distant. He wasn't. And besides, that's just *psychology*, which Wesley and I feel is fine, if you're Jewish, depressed, and a woman, in Vienna long ago. But in New York, now? Look elsewhere for answers. And good luck finding them.

So my dad said to me, or muttered, "Chinatown?" Which is both code and itself, too; it means, should we get away for a little while, the two of us? And it also means, let's go to Chinatown. He said something I couldn't hear to my mom, my mom got up and hugged me, I kissed my grandma good-bye, and my dad and I left together. We walked, even though there was a little rain. I'm actually, secretly, a little tired of Chinatown, and might have chosen somewhere else for us to hang out together, but I went because it seems my dad feels in control there, as he believes he knows how to order in Chinese. Once, after he'd rattled off this Chinese stuff, I saw our waiter go back to the kitchen, point at my dad, and say a few whispered Chinese things to some other waiters. They all laughed, and stopped when I stared them down. I never told my dad that, though; people need to believe what they believe about themselves, is how I see it, even in restaurants.

So we went to the Excellent Dumpling House, which despite its name has an intrinsic modesty. My dad told me about this buddy of his, named Joe. I'd never heard him say *buddy* before, ever. Joe, my dad told me, was the first actual gay guy he ever knew. He got to know Joe in the service, and was proud to say that even though it was a different time most of the other guys in the platoon thought Joe was pretty great, too. Now, I don't think my dad was ever in the service, actually, but it was still nice of him to bring gay Joe into our evening, whether or not he was real.

Then we discussed sex. He told me sex was beautiful, or it could be, and while he, personally, didn't know all that much about the gay aspects, he could never understand why most guys found it nauseating when who was it hurting, really? The food came, and we switched our focus from sex to scallion pancakes, duck with sour cabbage noodle soup, and Sizzling Beef Chow; I've taught myself to remember what I eat, as Wesley says he's learned from his time in the restaurant world that when people ask you how you've been, at least in New York, what they really want to know is what you've eaten recently.

We were eating when my dad put down his chopsticks and told me I was his best friend, and I should always know that. After we ate we walked around Chinatown for a while, sometimes just walking, not talking, sometimes telling jokes we'd each recently heard. My dad's funny, although not as funny as he thinks. Most people, I find, think they're funnier than they are, for reasons which may lie deep in what the really famous psychologist Carl Jung called *the collective unconscious*, even though I doubt there were comedy clubs there.

But who knows? No one. We went home, where me and my mom and dad talked some more, where Fartemis came to kiss me goodnight and give me some articles she'd printed out about Neil Patrick Harris and rates of HIV infection in Africa. I knew I was lucky, and appreciated it all. And still, I don't know why, but I wished they'd been, just maybe, just a little upset. I don't mean to the point where I'd have no choice but to run off and be a male prostitute in Seattle or anything, and not go to a good college, or any one, for that matter. But just a little, a *little* upset.

So I get to school, the day after my win, meeting Wesley a few blocks away, like always. We have our Facts, as usual, and by coincidence they're on the same subject, which is torture, which seems appropriate for the start of a fresh day of tenth grade. Wesley's fact is about this thing called flaying, where a guy, usually Japanese, slices off strips of your skin until you die a horrible death. My fact is about the ancient practice of Death by a Thousand Cuts, where a guy, also usually Japanese, cuts you a thousand (obviously) times until you die (again) a horrible death. It's not like we think these are good things; it's more that we're intrigued by Man's Inhumanity to Man, with a special focus on Asia.

We go into school. Some people and a few teachers congratulate me on winning, although I notice no one's running up and down the hall saying, "I'm gay!" in emulation.

"I have another one, too," Wesley says. "Too good to wait for. Also Asian, also torture, but more insidious. So in China if the Communists arrested you, and they arrested everyone, they sent you to a labor camp where you had to smile all the time. *Literally.* Have you ever tried to smile for more than a second?" He smiles, holds it. "Try it—"

"So did you talk to your dad?"

"More to George, really."

"So, what did he say?" George is Wesley's dad's partner. He's okay, mostly; when he talks to you he doesn't have that I'm Talking to a Young Person and Not Condescending to Them face. If you say something boring, he pays you the respect of actually looking bored. Wesley doesn't know if George and his dad are going to get married, even though his dad is always fighting for the right for Gays to do so and helped make it happen in New York. The Gays; that's one thing I'm a little nervous about, being part of a capitalized group all of a sudden, like the Hmong or Sioux or Abstract Expressionists, whom my mom's writing a book about.

"Well, I asked both questions," Wesley says. "And George needed till tonight, so he could think about it."

"What about your dad? What did he say?"

It takes him a minute to answer. He looks at me as if he's forgotten what I asked or isn't sure who I am. "He wants to think, too," he says finally.

"Well, that's a lot of thinking."

"Dude, I'm just quoting."

"You looked like you were about to say something," I say.

"Oh. Right." He laughs. "Like you'd know that."

What I want to say is: *I would. Because we know those things about each other; we always have.* And up till yesterday I would have said it, but I wouldn't have needed to, either. But—Obvious Guy, here—yesterday was then. And I wonder how many people in this hallway, right now, are thinking that besides me. And I know the answer.

Wesley looks down the hall, and I turn to see what he sees: Shannon Traube, looking at us, saying something to her campaign manager, Elspeth Grobman, who's looking at us, too. And I see Morgan

Blatt looking, and Jake Breslow, who says something to Donatella Gould, and just as I see them looking they look away, like they know a secret about me, although that would be hard as now I don't have any. Maybe there's one I don't know about yet; maybe they've found out about it first.

"Well, that's not a whole lot of help," I say.

"Sorry," Wesley says.

"Me, too," I tell him, and I don't know why.

Then all of a sudden Jake Krantz punches him on the arm, and Jake Kuperman, and Jake Blau, and he punches back and they're all laughing (literal laughs, not like ours); I didn't know they were friends. Wesley says, "I'll text George. He'll have something." And then, just like that, the hallway's empty and I'm the last one left.

So the day passes and I'm aware of all the minutes, fat and lazy as flies in a summerhouse. I see Wesley a couple of times, but he hasn't heard anything back from George. Nineteen years later we're on the bus to soccer practice, going to this field a lot of schools use in the park. When we get off the bus Wesley and I kick the ball around for a while, not saying anything, just doing it. I'm better at scoring and passing, he's better at dribbling and defense. All through the park, from different schools, boys and girls are doing just what we are; an alien, looking down from his space ship, would report to his leader that Earthlings chase white spheres, sometimes kicking them and sometimes bouncing them off pathetically small heads. They'd think this is how we fight our wars and decide not to conquer us, as it's well documented that aliens have no feet.

"So did you text George?" I say.

We're at the goal and I'm the goalie, I guess. Wesley nudges the ball a little.

"I did," he says.

"And?"

He kicks the ball in, hard. I leap, catch it, take it onto the field with this series of interesting moves I've worked on at home for like ninety-three hours, time that might have been better spent, probably, honing my Individuality for application stuff next year. Reza Aliaabaadi's dad, who comes to every practice, screams at him in Farsi; his grandpa was the shah of Iran's eye doctor, apparently, so they're a fairly bitter family.

"I didn't hear back," Wesley says.

"But I thought you said you would. You were like *sure*."

"George isn't *required* to text back, like he was my dad, or anything. He's not; he's no one. In the actual sense."

"No one's no one."

"Ha."

"What?"

"You know who said that exact same thing this morning? My dad."

"So he did say something, then," I say. "And yet you said he wanted to think. So which was it?"

"So what did you and your dad do in Chinatown?" he says.

I just go with it. "We had scallion pancakes," I say. "Sizzling beef *chow fun*. It was all good. So you said your dad—"

"That's what you *ate*. I mean what did you talk about?"

"We walked around. He said I was his best friend. So you said—"

"My dad," he says. "Yeah." I pass him the ball, watch as he does his own set of moves. "He doesn't like Chinese food."

It's starting to get dark, so I can't see his face too well, but I can tell he's not himself; sometimes, when you know a person, you don't have to see their face to know that.

"He does, too!" I say. "We had it that night at your house, when we watched *Top Chef. Lo mein,* and *kung pao* scallops—"

"The *kung pao* was shrimp," he says. "And that wasn't my dad, incidentally. It was George. They're not the *same*."

"Ha," I say. "Good to know. Because I might have been misled into *thinking* they were, both being gay guys."

"He couldn't get home that night."

"Where was he?"

"*I* don't know," he says. "Being invaluable somewhere. Which must make having me there really suck."

"What do you mean?"

He now does what he saw me do with the ball, and does it well. Wesley picks things up fast; he's observant.

"Forget I said it," he says.

"But you did," I say. "So I can't."

I wait for one of us to say, *Obvious Guy,* which is what we'd usually do. But we don't, and I wonder if he knows that, like I do.

"You know what your problem is?"

I didn't know I had one. Not that I'm perfect; I've got lots of faults. But with me and him? Well, it's another first, as it's also a first for me to be suddenly wanting to hear it. "What?"

"You remember too much."

"You know what yours is?" I say. But I suddenly feel I'm in a jar, shrunk to a tiny but anatomically proportionate version of myself, that even if I said what his problem is no one could hear me anyway. And besides—I can't think of one for him; all I can think of are mine.

Practice is starting. Reza's dad screams louder, only at Reza, fortunately, who gives him the finger and tells him they're not in Tehran, while moms on cell phones tell maids what to do about dinner. "Evgenia is going through a gnocchi phase," I hear one say. "Which you're well aware of, Corazón." I can't stop noticing things, or hearing bits of other people's lives; I feel like I'm up a tree, hidden by leaves, and if most of me were to vanish like the Cheshire cat what would be left, in my case, is not a smile but an eye that never closes and an ear sharp as a dog's.

"I gotta get in the game, okay?" Wesley says, tossing the ball back to me. "That's why we're here."

"I know that," I say. "I want to get in, too."

But we'll have to wait; our coach, which has been Jared Zam's dad since he lost his job, puts up a hand to stop us. As we wait, as it seems to be getting darker faster than it ever has, for the first time I feel scared. I didn't yesterday, when I made my speech and came out, but I do now. But—Obvious Guy again—yesterday was then.

Mr. Zam blows his whistle and calls our names. "I thought I was your best friend," Wesley says as we run out onto the field.

"You are!" I say. "I'm just telling you what my dad said! Which is more than you seem able to do!"

"Oh, I can do it," he says, as we make our way into the scrimmage. "Believe me."

"Well, at last."

"He said no," he says, as he keeps running, out into the dark field. "He doesn't think it's a choice."

"Just no? That's all?"

Mr. Zam is blowing his whistle again, shouting our names, telling us to get in or get out. We stay in, running now.

"It is," he says. "Because he also said that a thing can't be a choice if no one would ever choose it. That sounds like an answer to me."

"Me, too," I say, which is all that comes to me at first. "What did he mean, do you think?"

"I don't know!" he says. And as he's shouted it, and that's exciting to people, some boys drift to where we are, hoping more shouting will follow. "Figure it out!" But he doesn't wait for that. "He meant who would *choose* to mess up their life and be this fucked-up fag!"

"He said that?"

"I don't know!"

"But you were there," I say. "Sorry. Obvious Guy. But you were there."

"I don't know why I'm there," he says. "I walk in a room, he walks out. I say 'Good morning,' he suddenly has to go find something. I say, 'How are you,' and then—every time, like magic, practically, before he can tell me his phone rings." He acts it out, becoming his dad. "*Oh, shit, Wes, sorry, gotta get this, blah blah, fag, dyke, tranny . . . Wes? You're still here? Tell him how I am, George, I'm dealing with crucial significant gay stuff . . .* And maybe *that's* it, why I'm there, that is. To find his phone, and hand it to him, to understand when he has to take it because any person would."

"But I thought you said—"

"I didn't say anything!" he says. "So forget I said it."

He takes off, into the game, where I see that he's suddenly awesome. When did he get so good? He's better than me, which he wasn't two days ago; one more new thing in this day that's full of them. I try to get in the game, too, but Mr. Zam shouts to me to sit it out. I find a practice ball, work on my move, and just as I'm thinking how good it is I suddenly think: *Don't do this. Don't let anyone see. Stand very, very still.* And it's more than thinking; I *hear* those words, in a whisper. And I do what they say, which is the newest thing of all.

I never get in the game. On the bus back to school Wesley sits with Jake Kuperman, who has a Stradivarius he never plays, and Jake Krantz, who sells Adderall. I sit by myself, which is new. My locker is in the basement; they put some of us down there this year because some parents got worried that the halls were too crowded in case of a fire. I see no one has painted *Fag* on my locker, which would be terrible, obviously, and wouldn't speak well for Youth today, or at least Youth in our school. But I still wish someone had tried *something*. I'm not sure why, which worries me; I usually know the why of things.

I hear someone coming down the stairs, think I recognize the step, and find out I'm right; it's Wesley, with a soccer ball, doing the move he saw me do in the park. From upstairs, from the auditorium, I hear gunshots and singing; they're rehearsing *Assassins*, which is the fall musical.

"Would you show me something?" he says, capturing the ball with his foot and gently sending it over to me. "I keep fucking it up in the same places, for some reason. I want to make sure I'm doing it right."

"It's this," I say, showing him.

"That's all?"

I send the ball back and he's got it, perfectly, and the chance I didn't get in the park I get down here; we play our own game in the hall, so I guess everything's all right again.

"I have a Fact," he says. "A leftover one, but too good to not use."

"Do it."

"During the Ottoman Empire, they had these assassins? And what they'd do to them is break their eardrums and cut out their tongues, so they'd hear no secrets and couldn't tell what they saw."

"That's pretty imaginative, in a barbaric kind of way," I say. "And it introduces a new culture, which is also good."

"Yeah, I thought so. I have some others, too."

I put up my hand, to stop him.

"What?" he says.

But he stops talking; he trusts me; he gives me the quiet I need. Because I know something that's close to happening, and I need to listen. I don't have to wait long. It comes first as footsteps; sneakers, squeaking. Are they New Balance, maybe? My dad and I ordered pairs, online; we chose the colors; shipping was free. More footsteps now; someone else, and then someone else again; three now. "Did you hear that?" I ask, not because I'm unsure but just that it feels like the right thing to do. "Yes," he says, as the lights go out. And in the dark I think of things, one after the other, each of them separate and clear. *Monsters, Inc.*, how it was the first DVD I ever owned; my grandma's old hips, and what did they do with them; Micah Kinzer's hands, which I've never thought of before. I think of facts for our Fact-a-Day, and how now might be the time to share one.

But then I hear some words. Loud or quiet; I don't know.

Get the door.

Do I know the voice? I don't. But maybe I don't try too hard to know it, as I know it doesn't matter.

"Who's there?" This is Wesley. "Put the fucking lights on."

It stays dark, though, as I know it will; I know stuff, suddenly, that I've never known, all of it coming at me like text bells, loud ones that startle you but that are also helpful, in a way. Like I know what I'm going to hear next, the next word, like I could cue them if they forget. *Faggot.* I almost say it with them. Will a second voice say it? Yes. Then a third, the difference being that this one says, *Fag.* One syllable. Like cigarettes in England, where I went last summer on a teen tour.

"Who's there?" Wesley says again. Which even as he says it

seems more like something I'm remembering, from far off; as if it had happened, as if we were long past *now* and being here and reminding ourselves of it. When I get shoved, kicked, punched all over it's the same; the far-off thing. As it is when I'm lifted, held there, punched again. *It kept getting worse*, I think; again, like I was looking back, or reading a story about myself. Like when I fall, too, feel the concrete against my cheek and my body flipped, turned, hit with something; an object now, not just a fist.

But then it stops. I'm here again, sure of certain things; that this is my school, that's my friend, that we're in the middle of something sudden happening to us both. And what's next is seeing words, glowing, in different bold fonts, turning and spinning and floating. They're words *I'm* making, I know that, that I'm sending out for Wesley, who it seems is over me and holding me and shouting my name so maybe he misses the words I've sent.

So I read them, out loud, it seems, so he doesn't miss them. *Go* is the first word. Then: *They want* **me**. And then: *Really. Thank you. But this is* **mine**.

6.

Lenny

We met at Camp White Way, me and George, at twelve. That summer we played gamblers in *Guys and Dolls*, Cockneys in *My Fair Lady*, the only Siamese children in the history of productions of *The King and I* who were also, soon, to be *Bar Mitzvah* boys. At eighteen we reconnected in a tour of *Les Mis*, where we both played Revolutionaries without ever knowing why we were supposed to be so darn agitated, aside from the show not being very good. We kept this up, in this show and others, until we were both twenty-five, sharing an apartment on Ninth Avenue, supplementing our income with Bottled Free-Trade Artisanal Chutney. One day we looked at each other and, simultaneously, said, *Fuck it*, end of dream; cue real life.

So we're here now, in that other form of urban theater: *restaurants*. We're doing okay; not *well*, because no one is, but well enough to keep the lights on, low, at a flattering level. And we want to stay here; this theater district means something to us both. I remember our Saturdays thirty years ago, when we'd meet to slip into the second acts of flops. Times Square was still disgusting then, and fabulous; its true squalor may have already started to fade, but there was enough left to get the idea. People were still furtive, and wore hats. I miss hats and furtiveness; maybe they'll return, with the *World-Telegram.* I'm waiting.

I walk through Times Square, round the corner, and make my way up Eighth Avenue. George has called this morning, asking me to come in early, which he never does. As I turn on to Forty-seventh I Gene Kelly my way around a lamppost and hop down the brass-edged steps that lead from the street to the restaurant, where I see all the chairs are on tables, like flappers. As I come in George sees me and steps out from the kitchen. I can't read his face; why does he want me here? He bears, as always, a gift, a warm ham-and-cheese croissant, and then he takes down a chair and signals me to sit.

"Thank you," I say.

"Enjoy," he says, which we both hate and never say. Then he looks at me like he knows me too well, which he does. "Don't tell me. It didn't go well last night, did it? What was his name? Tyler, maybe?"

I burn my tongue on the croissant's lava-like filling. "Taylor. And I should have known it would be a disaster. It always is now, when you don't meet on the Internet but on the actual street. I don't want to *meet* people. I just want to read about their characteristics, in a profile. And then judge them." I take another taste. "Harshly."

"Was he cute, at least?"

I quote Frank O'Hara, in words culled, years ago, from a poetic but faithless boyfriend. "'It is easy to be beautiful,'" I say, "'but difficult to appear so.'"

"And was he beautiful?"

I am terrible; I am shallow. "He had a finger," I say, "that was deformed."

"There's always a finger," George says. "Somewhere."

"And he has a one-man show."

"I'm sorry. Did he do it for you? Was there abuse in it? Mormons?"

"It was about the Bauhaus. He does all the members, with the German accents. His Oskar Schlemmer was amazing, by far the best I've ever heard—"

"Lenny," George says. Just that, my name, which is how I know he didn't call me in early for good news.

"I knew it," I say. "I'm psychic. We're closing, right?"

"What are you talking about?"

"George. Come on." I sweep my arm through the air, to take in the pleasant little kingdom we've built over the past decade. "It's dead. You can say it. That's why you wanted me in early, to break it to me."

"No!" George says. "And since when are you psychic? I just need to ask you something—"

"Phyllis, in *Follies*," I say, stopping him before he can tell me; it's an Actor Thing, done for luck: when a fellow actor wants to ask you something, you answer right away with the character you most wish you could play; the idea is that, someday, you'll get a chance to play it. I've left the stage, but I want to keep my options open.

"This isn't that," he says. "It's this: When did you know?"

Ah. We are men, of an age, in a city that both is much like New York and is New York, so this question must mean when did I know I was (*whisper*) (*you know*) (*gay*). How can we have been friends for so long, I wonder, and never have gotten to this? This used to be *the* question, back in the great dead *then*, in the days before knowledge had turned into *information*. *Forever*; that was an answer. Or *sophomore year*. Seeing some tragic star on tv, her pain and talent so powerful that she could reach out from the screen, grab an impressionable boy by the neck, and make him hers, for life. Whereas today . . . well, enough about today. "Why?"

"Someone asked."

"About me, personally?"

"No."

"Who was it?"

"Wesley."

"Really? Do you think that he might be—"

But George doesn't let me get out the word, the one I was going to whisper, anyway. He shakes his head, as Armando butts in with a plate of artichoke risotto; the balances were off, subtly, on Saturday night, and George wasn't happy. George tastes it, as do I; we're happy, and Armando goes back to the kitchen.

"His friend is," George says. Then, in a whisper: "*Gay,*" he says. "Remember the kid who came in alone last week? Ginger ale, spaghetti with butter? He came out in school. And because Kenny and I are—you know—" It's now, somehow, even harder to say the word. I try to help.

"What? Democrats? North Koreans? Tory voters? Help me, a little."

"This kid wanted Wesley to ask me and Kenny some *questions.* Including the *when did you know.*"

"What did you say?"

"I couldn't think of anything," George says. "Like suddenly I had no history. I asked if we could talk about it later. So you think about it, too. I'd really appreciate it." He turns to scan the scorched earth of our reservation book. "Light night." He's on his way to the kitchen when it comes to me, easily. I reach for his arm.

"What?"

"I don't have to think," I say. "I can tell you now."

"Okay."

"Flipper." As I say his name I can sense him, here in the room with us, cheerful, meaty, gray. George looks puzzled, which I can't understand, as it's so clear to me. "The question you just asked me! That's my answer! I knew, from Flipper."

"I'll tell Wesley. Now, I have to try that risotto again."

But I take his arm again, to stop him, to tell him. And as I do I'm eleven again, nuzzling twelve, in that string of Saturday nights; my parents are out, my brothers and I are in the den, and my grandma is at work on one of her needlepoint pillows of Jewish Giants of Show Business. We're waiting for *Flipper,* me most intently, despite the fact that by 1980 the show is reruns of reruns from the mid-'60s, ghosts of itself. The show comes on, with its two motherless boys, its hirsute dad, and Flipper, the shimmering friend. I'm a year or so from figuring out that I'd happily replace him as friend to the older one. What I do know, for sure, is that I want passionately to be with them in Florida, in the Keys or the Glades or wherever such goyim live.

So one night, I say, I'm almost asleep. I turn to the window, and there's this large *face.* Flipper's. Smiling. He tells me to hop on. Then, just like that, we're skimming along the surface of the ocean. He laughs, and then, in a cloud of shpritz, shoots up into the air, comes down, and dives under, through universities of fish, until we come to a great set of gates that open to reveal a town. Then Sandy, the golden older brother, swims forth and says, "Lenny! Welcome. We've been waiting for you." He offers his hand, and even down here, where there is no sun, some sort of light catches the gold of the hair on his forearms. Then Flipper expands to a hundred times his usual size, opening his smiling mouth to reveal a beautiful room. And as Sandy and I start to swim in together—

"That's when you knew?" George says.

"I guess so," I say, because I see that now.

"You want to add anything?"

"Well," I say, "once we're inside—"

George puts up a hand. "Send me the link," he says, which is our code for *I've just stopped paying attention.* He straightens a few posters of forgotten flops; life, according to our walls, is a place where all hopes die and nothing works out. "So I might have to ask you to cover for me tonight. There might be some stuff, upstairs."

"That's fine. Could I just ask one question?" He doesn't say no. "Why don't I like Kenny?"

"I don't know," he says.

Neither do I. He is handsome, necessary; he's made a difference in the lives of thousands of gay people, and not just the cute ones. "Is it because he isn't funny?"

I have to give George credit; he considers what I've asked, as opposed to just slugging me. "Maybe," he says, "it's that you're not as funny as you think you are, and he's funnier than you know. Because you can't know, right? About how anyone is, when they're alone with the person they love." He brushes some dandruff from my shoulder, even though I don't have any. "I wish you liked him. He knows you don't. So. Calamari? Any thoughts?"

This is a daily question, as calamari is a signature dish. We stuff it, fry it, braise it in a stew. "Grilled?" I say. "We haven't done that since last Monday, and it sold."

"Yes." He likes this; we're a good team. "In a salad. With baby scallops."

"Smaller," I say. "Newborn."

He doesn't laugh, and I didn't intend him to; a small joke at the right time can act as a miner's light in the cave of a friendship, a search for what's in the dark. And I know something is; I know George; I hear it, whatever it is, breathing.

And I'm right. "Kenny's getting an award," George says; he may not know this is the start of something, but I do. "Even though you don't like him." He takes down some chairs, centers a cruet, shuts his eyes and sniffs to make sure the right aromatic balance found between Forty-seventh Street and Tuscany; we have a story to tell here, every day.

"When isn't he getting one?"

"And Wesley needs us," he says. "He said so, just flat out." He takes more chairs down, setting them just so; he holds a water glass up to the light, turning it, in search of fingerprints. "He needs Kenny, that is." This glass has passed inspection; on to the next. "His dad."

"I know who Kenny is." I help with the chairs, help to make a beautiful room. We've had a light past few weeks, so each day we stage the floor is a statement of faith. We move past each other, easy in our choreography, doing our jobs and silent for a while.

Then George continues. "Because there was something else Wesley asked this morning," he says, answering a question I haven't asked, one that he's put to himself, it seems. "If we thought being gay was a choice. And Kenny didn't even have to think about it. He said no, almost before Wesley could even finish his sentence. He said—who'd choose a life that would be like this?" George gets a text, which startles him. He takes out his phone but doesn't read the message; he just turns the phone in his hand, breathing on it, polishing it. Then he looks at me. "He was so sure. And I usually love that. But isn't it my life, too? I thought, *Do I know* any*thing? Do I know this man?*"

The reservation line rings, which is good, which means business.

Caller ID tells me it's our stalwart, Mrs. Engler, who wants me to reassure her for the thousandth time that the osso buco is tender today. As I do that three more calls come in, then a fourth. As the last is from *Private Caller* I grab it first, as that can sometimes mean someone wonderful. I affect a slightly Italian accent. What if it's Angela Lansbury? It's not. It's a man, clearly calling from a noisy place, asking to speak to "Mr. George Seeger," and as he says this I realize it's been a long time since I've heard his last name, as in here he doesn't need one; he's just George. There are more calls now, a dozen emails from Open Table telling us of reservations for the next few days. Does this mean we're turning around? The theater is always the Fabulous Invalid; does that apply to theater district restaurants? I remember that I've got someone on the other end waiting for George. I turn, hand him the phone. Mrs. Engler calls back, this time for George, as he's the one whose tenderness meter she trusts.

"Mrs. Engler," I whisper, covering the receiver, but when I turn George isn't where I left him. He's in the middle of the room, in his coat, frozen in place.

"George?" I say. "Are you okay?"

"I can't find my scarf," he says.

I go into action, not questioning this, giving him mine. When I hold it out to him, though, he doesn't take it.

"Here's the thing," he says. "It's Wesley, see. That was the hospital. Something's happened."

7.

Jerry

We're crazy today. Well, all days, really. Give me your tired, your poor, your poorly dressed, as Hector, my favorite nurse, puts it. We have to take you in; we're the city. And, even with all this, I still pick this guy out of the crowd as he comes in, stepping into the light like an actor making an entrance. He actually was one, if I remember right, between stops on a tour of something. I could be wrong; it was a few hours one night, years ago, and somehow I am now *so fucking old.* But it's him; it's got to be. And will he know me? No way. He couldn't. Not here in the hospital, anyway. Because when someone winds up here they cross a line where they're not themselves, for a time. So you're not you, either.

"Excuse me," he says.

"Yes."

"There's a boy here. Two, actually. I got a call at work, this person said they'd been hurt."

"Name?" I act bored, busy; our workplace space psychologist

told us that flat affect actually helps people in distress, and he certainly seems to be.

"Wesley." He points to my computer. "Is he in there? His last name's Bowman, B-o-w-m-a-n. He's fifteen."

"Give me a minute here," I say. "I've been up and down all day."

"With what? Your mood?"

I laugh, although I see he didn't intend me to. And I make the choice to initiate CEC, which is what we call compassionate eye contact and which we're taught to use sparingly. "With my *system*. It happens all the time, we're actually pretty primitive here. Let's just give it a second. And you are—?"

"Me?" He seems surprised. "Oh, I'm not anyone. I'm—just George."

Yes, I think; *it's you*. I try to remember his last name. I can't. "So then you wouldn't be Mr. Bowman."

"Oh, no," he says, "his father is. Wesley's not my son. I'm—"

"Just George," I say, which I wouldn't have said if I didn't want him to remember me suddenly, to have pined for me all these years, here in this place where I'm not the hot-enough guy from twenty years ago but just a bureaucratic pain in the ass, hiding behind a computer.

He doesn't seem to have heard me, though. "George Seeger," he says. "The other boy's name is Theo."

"Theo what?"

"Shit," he says. "Sorry. But I don't think I even know it."

"That can happen. Things can get scrambled up in here. People forget the most important stuff about themselves."

He seems grateful for this. "They do?"

My screen pours out a few more facts. "Could his name be Rosen? I have a Theo Rosen, age fifteen."

"That's it. What's it say?"

"He's with an attending."

"So that must mean you have Wesley, too, right?"

"Yes. Here he is. Wesley Bowman." There's a picture, too, the facts of which I protect; blood, contusions, an eye swollen shut. And the other kid looks even worse. "He's also with an attending."

"Which means?"

What I do tell him: "He's with Dr. Singh." What I don't: cops have been here and talked with these boys, which I can only tell a parent.

"Singh?" he says. "That sounds good. It sounds musical. Is he a good doctor?"

"Well, he's young, so he touches people. They teach them that now."

The screen spills a little more, like a suspect being broken.

"It looks like they're both going to be held," I say. "For observation."

"But why?"

"It's standard in these cases." The word—*cases*—rattles him, I can tell, from the nod of the head and the quick smile that fades as fast as it comes. And I do something I never do; I tell him more about this boy, whom he's so quick to point out is not his. "Gay bashing," I say. "It's not always accurate, though, the information they give us here. We're just the first step in a process."

"I see. Of course."

"So you're not the father, then."

He's turning the color we call City Green, that comes from worry and waiting, under these particular lights. "Oh, no." He laughs, as if to suggest: How could that even be possible?

"Are you the guardian?"

"No, again."

"Family member—"

"I'm a friend," he says. "One might say." A few tears form, suddenly, and I'm surprised. I offer Kleenex, in a box decorated with starfish.

"These things are hard for anyone," I say. "You don't need a job description."

"It's what I *said,*" he says. "When I said 'one might say.' Because that's what he says, a lot. For a funny kid he can be pretty serious. He wants to sound like his dad." He lowers his voice, as if he's about to tell me a secret. "Whom I live with."

"Then you're his partner."

"Well," he says, "I guess. And I don't mean to be difficult, but he's a lawyer, who left a law firm? He could have been rich by now, maybe, but he's antigreed. He's been at the ACLU for a long time; he's a remarkable man."

"I'm sure he is."

"Really," he says, and I sense he's addressing himself. "So he doesn't like the word *partner.* It reminds him."

"What about you? What word would you choose?"

He seems surprised that I'd be interested, that anyone could be. "Me?" he says. "Whatever. There's no name for me."

We both turn as an old man, on oxygen, is brought in by Jesus and Arthur and moved to a gurney on which someone has left one of the *Twilight* books.

"What a mess," he says. "What a goldarned mess!" He reaches out, takes George's hand, his own bruised in that old-man way, with the marks of his last four PICC lines. "You're a gay, aren't you? My grandson Jared is a gay. We all benefit from the gays in our city." This gets applause; we are disproportionately represented, we gays, once you come through these doors. "But there's a limit!" he adds, as Jesus and Arthur bear him away.

Which is pretty much right when a woman comes in, with the breathlessness of someone who's ditched the cab five blocks back and run the rest of the way. George straightens up as he sees her, as she comes to him. I know, right away, who she is. "Well?" she asks George.

"He's with a doctor—"

But she doesn't let him finish; she turns right to me. "I'm the *mother,*" she says. *"And I want my son."*

A man comes in, and from how George moves to him I decide he's the dad. He nods to George and moves to the mother, already apologizing.

"I'm sorry," he says, not knowing she's beaten him to it by twenty seconds.

"I'm trying to get some information," she says, turning toward me.

Another man comes in now, and because I've gotten good at this after seventeen years I decide: *Second husband. Happy marriage. Deeply in love.* "Baby," the man says, and goes to her, shaking George's and the father's hands on his way. I see Dr. Singh, young and dark, and signal to him.

"Wesley's parents?" he says.

"Yes," says Mom, speaking for the team.

"He is a bright young individual," says Dr. Singh, who's a bright boy himself.

"Oh, yes," the mother says. "He always has been."

Second Husband offers Singh his hand. "Ben Korman. I'm a physician. But I know nothing."

And off they go now, these Approvables, the ones who get to go back. George starts to follow but stops himself, as if his muscles have learned to do that.

"Sorry," I say. "Rules."

"Of course."

"Have a seat," I say. "I've got a 1987 *Redbook* somewhere. And believe it or not, there's cake." And there is! We get a box of fancy leftovers each day from the place down the street, thanks from the all-organic baker whose finger we sewed back on.

"There should always be cake," he says, and I see now he's the most concerned of all of them. Like I say: seventeen years; people come in not knowing that this place turns them into little books, easy to read. "Maybe I should go."

"Give it a few minutes," I say. "Once the doctor comes out all the news moves pretty fast. And you're already here, right?"

Marlice, our head tech, beckons; it's Luz's birthday, which means cupcakes, and time for my break. I excuse myself as we gather in a bed bay for the birthday song, pulling the curtain around us. And as I see him through the slit, a still point at the heart of a dozen disasters, I remember how I met him, in the snow, in front of Saint Patrick's; he had chestnuts, I think, because I remember that right after our eyes met he offered me the bag. Then came "I'm George" and "I'm Jerry"; we talked for a minute or two, then he asked me over, for that night. And I went; you just said yes, then; people wanted you to.

He lived in Hell's Kitchen, I think. He cooked, a frittata, no fuss about it, just good. Then we watched a movie; I'm pretty sure it was *The Nun's Story*, with Audrey Hepburn, because that was the movie that made my Aunt Domenica decide to become a nun in the '50s. But, as I've learned to say now in most situations: *I could be wrong.*

"You don't remember me," I say. Break's over. I'm back to my screen.

"Pardon me?"

"It was a long time ago. Like maybe twenty years? I was blond, maybe? You were on tour, in some play?"

"Oh, my God," he says. "Wait . . . was it *Equus*?"

"That sounds right."

"I was a horse! Chip, the one who was good with fabrics. And it was snowing, right?"

"That's how I remember it."

"Well, I can't believe you remember *me*." He offers his hand. "I'm George."

"I know," I say. "We've been through that. Jerry."

"You've been great. I appreciate it." It's suddenly very busy, which he sees. He puts on his scarf. "Well," he says, "they won't need me. If you see him—"

"I'll say hey for you—"

"And that I know I owe him an answer. If it matters." He hands me a card, for his restaurant. "Come anytime. Please. As my guest."

A dazed, grief-stricken Hispanic man stumbles out from the back crying *"Mi amor! Mi amor!"* My screen offers one more fact, at the very moment my station floods with questioners, several of whom are covered in blood. "Wait," I call to him. He does. "I found you."

"What does that mean?"

I tap the screen. "You were in here, after all. The kid asked for you."

"He did?"

"When they brought him in," I say. "Yours was the name he gave."

He nods, thanks me; I don't even see him go as six more people have come clamoring for news. I do see the Remarkable Man, the father, alone, within earshot of us. Has he been there all along? Has he heard what I just told George? He sees me watching him, and he turns away.

8.

Lola

It's almost 4:00. The city is perilous today. A flood on the subway, a falling girder on Sixth Avenue, killing a therapist. Kenny is to my right, Ben to my left; I'm parenthesized by husbands. And George is here, too; our host, I suppose, as this place is his, although Kenny helped him buy it. Well, it's where Wesley wanted to meet. Not that he *wanted* to, or was in any way eager to talk. But he will, and *I* will, as that's my job today. It won't be easy—telling him it's time to come home, that this experiment of living with Kenny and George must end early; in fact, today. But it has to be done, and Kenny agrees. I wonder, as I look at George, if he really needs to be here, or should be; when Wesley asked if we could gather here I assumed George would absent himself, would understand that this is about our family, the one that is ended in some ways and, in others, can never be; the one that he can never join. But there he was, when I walked in, and what can I do? I could talk to Kenny; this isn't about sparing feelings but about moving forward, about what must come next. But he's here.

And Wesley's not. He went upstairs "for a minute," just before we got here; something to do with Facebook, naturally, that had to be dealt with *now.* It's always now; how can a fifteen-year-old be indispensable? And we all have places to be.

"Kenny?" I say. "This is crazy. You should go up and get him. Don't you think?"

Kenny, with what looks like a flicker of panic, turns to George, but before George can say one of his clever little somethings, Ben steps in.

"Give him a minute. He has to post coded messages, to other terrorists." He explains, to the others, "He's in a sleeper cell, a nice one, that has dances."

"He's kidding," I inform the table. "Although who knows what any of them do?"

Ben turns to Kenny now. "I saw you quoted in the *Times* this morning."

"Oh," Kenny says, "that was nothing. Just—" he air-quotes—"'gay stuff.'"

"And all this time, I never knew you were gay!" says Ben. Everyone laughs; it must have been necessary. Ben has a feel for that, when to come in and lighten things; I wish some of my authors had it, too. "So, tell me. Do you think you'll ever get all this marriage business through? On a federal level, I mean. Where it needs to be."

"I do," Kenny says, "but it's going to take time."

"It's around the corner," says George.

"We don't need to talk about this here," Kenny tells him.

But Ben does. "I always feel David, my son, would have married his boyfriend. But they couldn't even dream of it then. I see them, in my mind, raised on chairs. I think that's important, when this comes, that if it's two Jewish boys they're entitled to the traditions. The chair, the glass, the *chuppah*. Maybe not the sheet with the hole."

I take his hand, or he takes mine; there's so much more hand-taking in second marriages; it's often where sex begins. I was lucky enough to meet David. Ben and I fell in love so fast, within minutes, it seemed, after we met in the coffee shop by the hospital where he was visiting his dying son and I my dying father. Everything had to happen fast. Ben brought me to David's room. We talked a bit, funny stories about Ben. Then David, blind by then, asked me to read. I had the *New Yorker* with me, as always. I read a Jhumpa Lahiri story about a family, far from home, trying to find their way in a new country. The next day, David died, with Ben there, talking to him.

We are all texted at once. "Wesley?" I ask, but the general answer is no. I'm becoming more angry, and more worried, too. "Did you talk to him at all?" I ask Kenny. "Did he say anything?" Wesley didn't want to come with us after they released him; I didn't push it, although I could have.

"He knows this girl."

"Really? Who?" He knows lots of girls, of course, but has never mentioned one specifically.

"Shannon something."

"Traube," George, who always knows what Kenny doesn't, says.

"God, that's an awful name," I say. "What did he say about her?"

Again, Kenny looks to George. "I asked you. Not George." I turn to George. "I'm sorry, but—""

"No worries," George says, an expression I can't bear and have asked Wesley not to use.

"He talked about her yesterday, before it happened."

"Nothing last night? He didn't tell you who might have done it?"

"No."

"Did you ask?"

"It didn't seem like the right time."

"Which makes sense," I say, and I think, How am I suddenly the expert on the subject of a son getting beaten up in the basement of his school, one where media barons send their sons and daughters, one that preaches tolerance and earnestness and service to the community, where such things do not happen? My comment seems to have caused a silence to descend. How odd this is, I think, as I add up the five of us, in search of a sum; me, two husbands, a husband's boyfriend, and, of course, an absent pummeled boy; how odd to *feel* odd that there is something wrong in taking note of all that.

"So," Ben says, after a few more silent, awkward moments, "which of you two is the woman?"

"Enough," I say. "I'm calling him." I look at my phone, which, although it was fully charged an hour ago, shows the frightening battery with its stump of red; the reminder, as a colleague says, of the death of all things, ourselves included; the memento mori in our pockets. Before I can say anything, George is there to help me.

"I can get you a charger," he says. "We keep them here, for customers, for emergencies."

"Well, this *is* one. Thank you."

"Or I could go up and look for him."

I don't want that; I'm not sure why. "That's not necessary, George. Really."

He looks to Kenny. "Or you could?"

Kenny offers his phone to me. "Use mine."

I take it, and see that his screen saver is of George, younger, onstage in a role; his eyes look heavily made up, like a courtesan's, and he holds a glass unicorn in his hand. Although the picture is chaste I feel as if I've come across some secret about them. I press in numbers, anyway. "Nine one seven—"

"One quick thing?" George says.

"What?"

"That may not work."

"Well, that's too bad. It's going to work. It has to."

"He doesn't have his phone."

"Did he lose it?"

"No."

"Then where is it?"

"I have it."

"But why?"

"He ran up a bill. I lent him the money to pay it."

"Did you know about this?" I ask Kenny.

"No. You know how busy—"

"I'll send you a check, George."

"I'll give you a check," says Kenny.

"We made a deal. He's working off what he owes me down here. He has two hours left."

"What do you pay him?"

"Twelve an hour."

"Ha! We don't pay our editorial assistants that. What do you have him doing?"

"Prep. Plating. Torching. He fires the crème brulée tops. For the crackle."

"Is that safe?"

More texts drop, from some sky, for all of us; I return Kenny's phone to him as I see mine, glowing and alive from its charge. We tap back our responses, mine being *Good!*, one word in answer to my assistant's news that an author has just delivered a manuscript that is nine years late. As the men's fingers fly, as we await Wesley's return, I calm myself with a private recitation of my CV. I am Louise Farmer Bowman Korman, Lola since I was a girl, loved by my husband, able in my field. I am a member of PEN, executive editor (on hiatus) of the *Willa Cather Quarterly*. I am the mother of a boy who has always excelled at school, at sports, in friendship. And now, in less than a full day, I'm someone whose child is held for observation, mumbles *fine* when I ask how he is, lets me know my concern is a burden and an annoyance.

Then I see him. He's in the sweatshirt he was wearing when it happened, advertising some group I've never heard of; it's red, but you can still see where blood has crusted and dried. He has twelve stitches over his right eye, which looks twice as puffy and swollen as it did yesterday, multiple abrasions, and a broken left index finger, in a splint.

"Wesley?" I say, as if there were some chance it might not be him, that none of this has happened and the past twenty hours could be reclaimed.

"Hey."

All fingers freeze, midtext. "Hey," we all say.

"Finish your texts," he says, with a gracious sweep of a swollen, purple hand. "It's cool."

"Join us," I say. "Please. We've been worried."

He slowly approaches and, still standing, snatches a piece of bruschetta from the platter. He needs a haircut. That's what I think first, hating myself for thinking it. And he smells, too. Boys do, I know; a friend with boys says it's from their long race to manhood.

But this strong? Like one of those boys they find in France, who have lived in forests, raised by bears.

I give him a moment to crunch and chew, which looks like it hurts him. "This is good," he tells George, with his mouth full. "Just the right amount of garlic. Not overpowering." He burps and wipes his mouth with his sweatshirt, which I've never seen him do before. As he steps forth Ben gets up and holds out a chair for him. I feel myself relax. This can go well. No one needs to be hurt, or even upset. Don't charge. Approach. Gently.

But it turns out that what he wants is not a seat but a second piece of bruschetta, which he helps himself to and downs, more or less, without chewing. He grabs for a third, paces as he eats it, making muffled grunting sounds. I see him, midbite, gag, hunch over, and turn away from us.

"Wesley?" I say. "Sweetheart? What is it?"

"*Shit.*" As he turns back I see blood flow from his mouth. He guards something in his hand, the one that's purple and twice its size, not the one with the broken finger. "I thought this would happen," he says.

"Is it a tooth?"

He shows it to me, holding it out, watching my reaction. I've never actually seen a knocked-out tooth; dipped in blood, with the dangling root, it looks like a gory punctuation mark. "Let me have it," I say, as one might to a small dog, or child.

He just laughs. "No way. It's *mine.*"

"Does it hurt?"

"Hey," he says, with a knowing chuckle I've never heard from him, "this is what happens in fights. I mean, right?" He pitches this to the men at the table, and I'm grateful no one answers. I dig for a

Kleenex to give him, to wipe from his mouth the blood that makes it look as if he's just fed on some small, helpless something. But George is too quick for me. He's there first, with one of his rough, peasanty napkins dipped in water; as the light falls on him I can see he's started coloring his hair. Wesley puts the tooth in his pocket, wipes his face, returns the napkin. George gives it to a passing busboy. And that's it, no need of help from me. "Is there something that's like softer?" Wesley asks George.

"There's polenta? Flan?"

"Do you have the asparagus flan?"

"George?" I say. "Please. Don't bother."

"But I'm *starving.*"

"Just sit down first, with us. We've been waiting for you. Right, Kenny?"

He seems surprised. "Yes. Right."

Wesley doesn't sit, though. "I shouldn't be here, you know."

"Why not?"

"I'm missing Moral Imperatives. And one of the biggest moral imperatives is to always show *up* for Moral Imperatives."

Moral Imperatives is a requirement, meeting twice a week after school and intended to address, hopefully, the soul. "I think they'll understand, this once."

"No, they won't. Mr. Frechette says you have to have perfect attendance or you can forget Cornell. And that's a *safety* school." He turns to George. "Could I work tonight?"

"Do what your mom says, okay? Sit down."

He does. Whatever works. "Thank you," I tell George.

"No worries," says George, for the second time.

"*Ha,*" Wesley says sharply, as if he'd caught me doing something I'd denied but he knew I'd been secretly doing all along.

"What?"

"*He* can say that, but if I do—"

"George isn't my son. You are."

"So that means *I* can't say stuff that's like totally common parlans?"

Parlans. I'll fix that later. "Common parlance," I tell him, knowing even as I start that what I'm about to say I'd harshly judge if I heard it from someone else, "doesn't automatically suggest a civilized use of language. In fact, quite the opposite."

"And you're like the arbiter of civilization," Wesley says. "Like Nietzsche. Or Bellow."

Bellow? Then I remember. Ruth Lieber, across the hall from us, suffering from macular degeneration that Ben, who knows, says is hopeless; she paid Wesley to read *Seize the Day* aloud.

Ben, bless him again, saves me. "Can I take a look at your eye?"

As Wesley, for a moment, drops his swagger, I see how he lets Ben lay a soft hand on his shoulder. Ben, then, is safe, and easy. But at the hospital, when they pulled the curtain to reveal him to me, looking like this, seated on the end of a bed with his feet dangling, when I reached for him he flinched and slid quickly back.

"Look straight at me," Ben says. "Try not to blink." Wesley obeys. "Good. Like that. You're looking at sixty-four years of booze and whores, kid. Now to the left. And the right. No delusions that you're Steve and Eydie, or either, individually?"

"Who?"

"Then you pass. And we're done. By the weekend you should be pouting and glowering normally."

"Well, that's good news," I say. "And just to make sure this gets said, Wesley, thanks for joining us."

"Like I had a choice?"

This is not a question. It does not, therefore, need an answer. "We all know how awful this must have been for you."

"It wasn't."

Steady. "Well, you'd know. You're the one it happened to."

"And Theo, too."

"Yes. Also to him."

"And the guys who did it. 'Cause it wasn't like one-sided." He looks to the men again. "I can fight. Fortunately. The doctor said I was the lucky one, remember?"

"Who knows what he said? He could hardly speak English."

"Racist."

"Actually, I'm not."

"It's not an insult, Mom. It's just an observation."

"Wesley, if my racism helps you, then yes, I'm a racist."

"So you admit it."

"Because that's my one goal here, today," I say, "to help you. For all of us. It's why we're here."

"She's right, Wesley," Kenny says, surprising me. Wesley, startled, looks to him. I remind myself: he's a very effective man.

"I know," Wesley says quietly.

"Then let us help you."

"Well, here's the thing, which is no offense? I don't need it. And you're all like necessary incredible amazing people, who should be where you're needed. Not with me. What I need is to call Theo, and take a nap, and get my tooth put back in."

Necessary. Incredible. Amazing. Is this how he sees us? Is this how we are? "You can do all those things. They'll all happen—"

George cuts me off. "I called Theo," he says to Wesley.

I nod to him, in thanks. I think, *You shouldn't be here.* I *don't need* you.

"When?"

"Just before we all got here."

"How is he?"

"Tired. But he feels better. And he says *hey.*"

"I called him, too," I say. I didn't. I have known him all his life. Wesley looks at me, not with distrust, as he used to before these months here. The lie is too easy, which makes it worse. "I spoke to his mother, who said the same thing. They were watching *The Wire.*"

I have him. "Which season?" Wesley asks.

"Four."

"Well, that's the best one."

"Wesley, I think I know how you're feeling."

"You do?" The challenge is gone; the abraded jaw (increasingly Kenny's) no longer thrust out.

"I think. This happened to you together. Theo's your friend."

"Best," he quickly adds.

"Best. And what happened to you both should never have happened."

"But it did."

"And, thank God, you're the lucky one, as you said—"

"The *doctor* said."

"Yes. Which makes me sad for Theo, and his family."

"He's going to be okay, unless his mom told you something you're not telling me. Which you can tell me, if she did. I'm not a baby."

"I know you're not. And she didn't."

"I know more than you think."

"And while I'm sad for Theo I'm so grateful for you."

"Me? What did *I* do?"

"We're all grateful"—I nod, to his fathers, to Kenny, and Ben—"that you're not in some hospital bed, with a tv hanging in the air and terrible worries as to what might come next. Because we can figure that out here." Ben tries to take my hand but I keep it for myself; I need it, in case I have to reach for Wesley, if he'll let me, if it will help. "What comes next for *you*."

He says something, but I don't hear him. "Could you say that again?" I ask.

"I said, what if it was my fault?"

"But how would that be possible?"

"I could have fought harder. He could have gotten away."

I'm about to say something but, as with the blood, George is there before me.

"How can you even say that?" he demands aggressively, I think, even inappropriately. "How can you think for a second that that could be true?"

Before George can say more I say to Wesley, "Maybe you feel that now, and I'm sure it feels real. But keep in mind what you've been through."

"It's *in* my mind. It's keeping itself."

"And you'll see things differently later. I promise you."

"Which means?"

Take a breath.

"At the moment, you're not yourself."

There's a pause, one I don't like and know I've helped create. I regret what I've said, and I never do. It might just be that I'm worn out, too; I need to be that much more careful.

"I'm myself," Wesley says. "I'm always myself."

No one helps me. "I meant you're in shock." Will this end it?

No. "I'm not in shock."

"You are." What am I talking about? Do they still have shock? Does it still explain things?

"I'm not."

"You are. You got beaten up. Badly."

He laughs, pitching it to the men, as he did before. "I didn't get beaten up." He looks to Kenny. "Did I, Dad? You know about stuff like this."

This is mine, though. I don't let go. "You wound up in an emergency room. With twelve stitches."

"Ten. And what I got in was a *fight*. There's a difference. You probably don't know about stuff like that."

He's said this with a condescension that is, in its way, protective and even sweet. Maybe this is too much right now; Ben thought it might be. Tomorrow the weekend begins, and we'll have him, anyway. "You're right," I say. "I'm sorry."

"You're an *editor*. You should choose your words more carefully."

"*Hey*," George says quietly, but Wesley hears him and, as if enchanted, turns from me to him. "Don't do that."

"But she—"

George keeps his voice low. Am I hearing what I think I am? "Don't talk to your mother that way," he says.

Wesley whips his head back to me, shocked and grieved by the world's unfairness, the level at which he is misunderstood. "But when a person says a thing, and it's totally *not* what the thing is—"

There are a few people at the bar, but we don't seem to interest them. They are fixed, like everyone, on their phones and opinions.

"Don't talk to your mother that way."

"Sorry," Wesley says to him.

"Don't tell *me*."

"I'm. Sorry. Mom."

He doesn't wait for me to acknowledge this. He turns to Kenny, stops slumping, sits up straight in his chair. Kenny matches him. He waits for Wesley to speak. He doesn't, and we don't.

"Yes?" Kenny says.

This is my son; this was my husband. I haven't been between them for many years.

"Nothing," Wesley says; at last, I suppose. "Sorry."

Ben brings us back, with a nod to me. "Lo. You were about to say something about what comes next."

It's as if all the interruptions haven't happened. I have new energy, know just where I was—in midsentence, even—and where I want to be. "—that when you made this change we all thought it was a good idea, for you and your father. You could get to know each other much better than you ever could at restaurants, or movies, or—counting dinosaur bones." I have been delightful, on purpose, as George is. But it goes unmarked. "And it has been a good thing for these past two months." Wesley, I notice, still has his eyes on Kenny. "You're doing well in school. We miss you, of course—"

"Can I get anyone more bruschetta?" He's our host, suddenly, rather than our problem. "There's *checca*, and a puree of white beans, *con rosmarino*." In spite of the *Raging Bull* face he is elegant and gracious, two qualities I've never seen in him before. He reminds me of someone. Who? Yes. George. "We've also got some—"

"Let George take care of that," I say. George semaphores to Lenny, saying God knows what.

"Thanks," I say. "And it has been good, as I was saying—"

"What did you think, Dad?"

"I think you should let your mother make her point."

"But that's not an answer."

I try to help. "He thought it was—"

Wesley raises a hand to stop me. "Let him tell me, Mom!"

"All right," Kenny says. "I agreed with her."

"That it would be good?"

"I thought it would be fine."

"Wow. Hyperbolic."

Kenny, poised to explain, looks to all of us. "It's a New York apartment. It's a *box*."

"But that *is* New York!" George says. I sense he may have nothing beyond that, although he never loses the Broadway smile. "Boxes on *boxes*. Because when you're here, you—give up space. Right? For house seats . . . in the Theater of Life!"

"You should write," Ben says.

"But things have changed," I say, bringing us back. "Given what's happened."

Wesley echoes me. "Given what's happened."

"We need to decide whether your living here, and not with us, is the best thing for you right now." I'm girded, ready for him to come at me, but his focus is still on Kenny.

"Dad?"

"Your mother's right," he says. "We need to deal with this."

"*This* being *me*. Or the *concept* or *perception* of me. Phenomenologically. In the interests of clarity."

"That's an interesting discussion for later," I say. "When we settle this—"

"Who's 'we,' Mom?" For someone held for observation less than twenty-four hours ago, he's quick on his feet. "Who's 'we'?"

"All of us. We all want what's best for you."

"But what do *you* want, Dad?"

"You heard your mother, I think."

"I mean *you. Specifically.* Dad."

"Why would that matter? This isn't about me."

"Don't you want anything other than 'what's best for me'? Everybody wants *something,* Dad. Just tell me one thing."

"I'm not going to."

"Why?"

"This isn't *my* problem, unless I'm seriously mistaken."

"But, Dad? I just have to ask you one serious personal question," he says. "If that's okay with you?"

He seems to have calmed down. He even smiles a little, which makes his face look worse. But the smile has its effect. We're all lightbulbs now, glowing with encouragement; you could read by us.

"That's why we're here," Kenny says. "And why *I'm* here."

"Why do you let people call you *Kenny*?"

"It's my name," Kenny says. He turns to us. "Isn't it?"

We agree, too enthusiastically, but I sense it's too late; Wesley flushes and seems almost, slightly, to ascend. "But it's not."

The sour smell of grievance, like the insides of sneakers, diffuses through the room. I have to do something, and feel that even more strongly as early diners come in and Lenny, stepping in for George, moves to welcome them. "Wesley—"

But he's made me invisible; I don't count. "*Kenny,*" he announces, "is a *boy's* name. Not a man's. He's a boy in a hood on *South Park* who keeps getting killed and who never dies. He's paper, all cut up—"

"Hey, Wes," Ben says, trying to help. But Wesley is up again, panting, as Kenny looks down, tightens his lips, perceptibly shakes his head to say, in steps: *No. I won't do this. Don't look to me for this.* I know those steps; each of them.

But Wesley doesn't. "Why, Dad?"

It's clear Kenny isn't going to answer. "All right," I say, although I don't know where to go next. I tell authors, *Write through it; write anything when you don't know.* Does that apply to sons? "You're fifteen." That's a start. His mouth opens in protest, but I press on. "A *mature* fifteen, in many ways. But that still doesn't make you sixteen—"

He pounces. "Which means—?"

"That someone needs to know—"

"Needs to know what?"

"Some responsible, concerned *adult* needs to know where you are at all times."

"People know!"

"And they need to know *what* you're doing, too."

"They also know that!"

"And just who, exactly, *specifically*, you're doing it with." I realize, again, that I'm doing all the heavy lifting. "Right, Kenny?"

"Lola—"

"Just let us know you fundamentally agree, so we know you're here."

"You know I do. More than fundamentally."

The door opens to let in four men, ageless, laughing, all in scarves that seem, even inside, to be blown by an ideal wind. One of them waves to George, but George doesn't wave back.

"Wesley?" I say. "Look at me." He does. I'm surprised. "How well do you know this Theo?" He laughs. "Is that an amusing question?"

"*This* Theo? You just like throw in the adjective *this*?"

Is *this* an adjective? "Just answer the question."

"He doesn't need adjectives, Mom. He's just a noun. He's *Theo*."

"I know who he is. My point is—"

"And you personally said—I heard you—that you think he's awesome."

"I'd never have said that."

"But you did."

"George Eliot is awesome." Again, I'm the person I'd condemn if I heard her say what I'm saying. "Iris *Murdoch*. Rebecca *West*."

"Who?"

"Women from the sisterhood," Ben says.

"Theo Rosen is—" I can't find what I want to say right away, which, of course, Wesley smells.

"Well? If he's not awesome, he must be something else," Wesley says. "You're great with words; you use them all day and help people win things. So he's—"

I'm trapped. "Creative."

"In other words," Wesley says, "gay."

"I didn't say that."

"You don't have to. Because he is. Like Dad, and like George. And like those Scarf Guys at that table. Not to racially profile, or anything."

I shudder, in an almost enjoyable way, as I feel words flow through me, startling and cool. "You used to have so many friends. But this whole past year all we hear is Theo this, Theo that—"

"She's right," says Kenny.

"Thank you," I say.

"What ever happened to that kid—? You know the one I mean. The amazing soccer player. Jake somebody?" Kenny turns to George. "Does that sound right?"

"Dad? All my friends are named Jake. Unless they're named Max. Except, of course, for Theo and me. But I'm not my friend."

"Jake Blau," I say. "What ever happened to him?"

"How would I know?" he says, about someone he sees every day.

"You're a great soccer player, too, right?" Kenny says. "That's how."

Wesley laughs. "Oh, no, I'm not."

"You are," Kenny and I both say.

"I hate sports."

"You don't," I say. "You're exquisitely coordinated."

" 'Exquisitely'?"

"You ski, you play tennis, you do track."

"You *run* track, Mom. And you don't mean Jake Blau. You mean Jake Greenspan. Who got bitten by a tick, in Quogue, who's near death."

"Oh, my God," I say, "how awful. I didn't know that. I should call his mother."

"It might not be so awful," Wesley says. "It might help at Yale. Death is a plus at Yale."

"Wesley!"

"We hear stuff like that every *minute.* Like you open your locker, a voice says, *Be interesting! Be varied!* And I talk about Theo because he actually *is.* He's like *avid*, about everything there is in life. Not so he could say, *I'm avid*, on applications but because he actually is. It's *who* he is. And it's how I'd like to be, and when we hang out I even am, a little. And you don't need to say any supportive stuff, or anything. I *have* self-esteem." He downs a glass of water, another, then a third, without even seeming to breathe.

I don't know what to say. "All right, then."

"So can I please go?"

I sense he's not the only one who wants that. How can I do this to him after what he's been through? But I have to. No one else will. "Does Theo come by after school?" I ask.

He looks straight at me, for the first time, and moves closer, too. As he does I see him in his crib, looking up at me while I looked down to him; how we'd do that for minutes at a time, how it seemed as if that could be all you needed in life. "How?" he says. "School's like *eternal*, there's no *delineations*, like when you were young."

And he's right. He's busier than I am, as they all are, because we've seen to that. It's only to keep them safe, and these things happen, anyway. "But that's not what I mean."

"Oh, I know that," he says gently, with what almost seems like tenderness. "What you mean is do we spend a lot of time together."

"Well?"

"In the afternoons. We do the same things, because we're basically the same person."

But you're not gay, I want to say, and don't. The scarved men laugh, at something Lenny, hovering, says to them. But they seem far away. "Do you see each other at night?"

"Lola—" Kenny says.

"Does he come for dinner, say?"

Wesley turns to George, as if they'd agreed upon an answer ahead of time. "I think he was there like a few weeks ago?"

"So it was the four of you?" I say.

"Just me and Theo," he says.

"Ah."

"And George."

And George. My spell with Wesley breaks as I call on Kenny. "You weren't there," I say.

"For one night," Kenny says.

"All right."

He offers more. "I was in Pittsburgh. One night."

"I wish I'd known," Ben says. "My Aunt Celia lives there. She's ninety-six, and blind. But she still makes her famous *flanken*. In the dark."

"It was one night."

"You keep saying that," I say. "What were you doing there?"

"Lo, it was nothing."

"It wasn't," George says. "He was Man of the Year for the Pennsylvania-Massachusetts Harvey Milk Society."

"That's not nothing," Wesley says. "You should be proud of that, Dad."

I'm moved by what Wesley has said, even as I wonder how often Kenny is gone; the point of this downtown sabbatical was for Wesley to have time with Kenny, and Kenny's not there? "So you and Theo were alone, then," I say to Wesley. "Without supervision."

"We didn't need it. We were writing papers, on Flannery O'Connor," Wesley says. "Did you know she had lupus?"

"Of course I did," I say too quickly. Me; the one I'd condemn.

"George read one of her books, too," Wesley says. "*A Good Man Is Hard to Find.*"

"It probably sounds stupid," George says. "But I read what he reads, sometimes."

"Why would you do that?" I say.

"I don't know," he says. "I'm dumb. I do it so I have something to say for myself. About something other than *Gypsy*."

"What are you talking about?" Wesley says. He's angry with George; I can see it. "You have plenty to say for yourself. So you shouldn't talk like that." I've never heard him talk like *this,* say something openly supportive to anyone before. When did that begin?

"Anyway," George says, "that night, they came down when they finished their homework and I gave them dinner."

"What time?" I ask.

"Nine?"

"But that's too late."

"So he comes for dinner," Ben says. "Lucky him. *I* would. And I'd like to say something, and then shut up. To do what this kid did, at fifteen? I've seen so much in life. And this, to me, is a flag on the moon." He raises a glass. "To Theo."

"And what's happened since then has taught us something," I say. I have to name that now, and I'm not sure I can. But it comes. I have it. And I have to share it; it can't just be mine. "That we don't live in a bubble."

Wesley is a game-show contestant, hand primed for the buzzer "Which means?"

I look from one man to the next. "Anyone want to help?" No one does. "It means a place," I say, "where you think you can live without reckoning. Without fear." Without my willing it, my hand extends to sweep around the room, to take in the five of us in here and the specific bit of city out there. "And this," I say, "is ours. Our bubble. New York, we're New Yorkers, it's the theater district—"

I see Wesley has moved still closer to me. "Which means?" he says.

"Just this," I say. "That we believe that everything, in our particular bubble—I wish I had a better word—is safe, and sure. But it's not." No one stops me, or plucks words to challenge or question; I almost wish they would. "And with Theo—"

"You have to stop for a second, Mom."

"Wesley—"

"I want to know what Dad thinks."

Kenny stays cool. "Look," he says, "I've said this already. I can keep saying it. Right now, here, *why* we're here is not about me."

"Who's it about, then?"

"You know something, Wesley? I don't like to say this, but you have become incredibly rude."

"It's rude to be asked a question and then not answer it. *That's* rude."

"I don't know what's happening to you," says Kenny. "I just don't." He turns now to me. "Could this wait till the weekend? You don't even know what I had to do to be here today."

"All you have to do is say who it's about," Wesley says.

Kenny bangs the table, which I've never seen him do. "It's about *you, goddamnit*! And this situation we're in, and what we need to do about it! And where you're going to live!"

"Where do you want me?"

Kenny bolts from his seat, flinging his hands up in the air, a surrender. "I'm not going to do this anymore. I *can't* do this."

George takes his arm, brings him back. "Kenny? *Try*. Please try."

Kenny looks down at George's hand, as if surprised to find it there. "Don't you *know* me?" But George's hand must have done something, for Kenny sits again, and in a moment it's as if nothing has happened. But something has to happen now, and I know what it is.

"Wesley?" I say. "Are you and Theo—" I don't even know what word to use; I don't want to scare him off. I look to everyone else, but their faces give me nothing. So I do the best I can. "Are you together?"

He seems to be smiling at me. I can't tell. "Do you mean are we boyfriends?"

The word sounds odd, coming from him; a toy word, with a wind-up key, not one that suggests something real, between people. "Yes," I say. "I mean—"

"In love," George says. He's tried to help me; I know that; or help Wesley, is more like it. And even though I know this I'm dizzy with rage. What I feel, in fact, is beyond that. I can't understand it. I don't have *words* for it. And I always have words.

"What do you think, Mom? I'm sure you think *something*. So you might as well say it."

"Wesley," I say, "I just don't know. I feel like I don't know anything." Then something happens that seems separate from me, like it was planned for me by someone else. I turn to George, who's right there, as if he'd been waiting. "But you do," I say to him. "I just know that you do." He doesn't answer, but he doesn't look away, either. And I see something, now, that I wish I didn't, about this man, facing me, whom I have known for a long time now to be unfailingly gracious and effortlessly kind. No, it's not about him; it's about me. What I see is that I don't trust him. Maybe I never have. I didn't know that until today, sitting here, at his table. But I know it now.

George nods to me with what looks like a very small smile. He knows what I'm thinking, I can tell. "I see" is all he says.

"You're with Wesley a lot, it seems."

"He hardly ever is, Mom—"

"Please let me talk to George, Wesley."

"But you're talking about *me*!"

"I'm with him *sometimes*," George says. "Not that much. Ten minutes in the morning, mostly. He's busy, for one thing; he's got his life. And I've got mine."

"He's upstairs, though. And Kenny's always somewhere. There's nothing to stop you from going up whenever you like."

"That's right. It is my home, for one thing."

"Have you done that?"

"A few times, maybe."

"Just maybe?"

"I'm sorry. No. Definitely. But not many."

"All right," I say. "Thank you." I look at Wesley, count his stitches. And he's right; there are only ten.

"And how do I know what happens when you do?"

He wants to make me comfortable. It's what he does, where his gift lies. "You just have to ask. I'll tell you whatever you want to know."

"Well, I'm asking. I'm sorry, George. But I'm asking you now." He looks to Kenny. Kenny looks down.

"When we're alone—" George begins.

I don't know if he'll go further. I jump in, edit; I know when, and how, to help things along. "Have you touched Wesley?"

"Mom."

I think that I'm not me; I'm no one I know, or would ever want to. But it passes. I have a job to do. "Tell me, George."

I'm out of my chair, not quite sure when it happened. Ben is, too, as is Wesley. But not George. Ben wants to bring me close; Wesley wants me to stop. I see that. But I have to do this. I don't have a choice.

"I have to know." I turn to the others, to make the case I don't even have to make. "I'm his mother. I have to know."

What surprises me is the noise, how sudden and loud it is (low ceilings? Or do they make things quieter?) and how quickly it grows quiet again. Dishes, glasses, silverware, all hitting the floor. Then, in the quiet, I hear ice cubes as they rearrange themselves in the one glass spared from Wesley's sweep of the table. I'm out of questions now, and I'm no longer looking at George. All I want is for Wesley to be safe; I don't think that's too much to ask. But as I reach for him he steps back, as far as he can in the small room, like a photographer who wants us all in the picture at once.

Then he goes, out the door, into the street, and I'd follow if there wasn't all this *mess*. I see Lenny, staying as far back as he can, trying to grant us our privacy in what's already, for tonight, a festive public space, this week celebrating, per the card on the table, the cuisine of Lombardy. But we can't stay here. Others will want this table, for before or after the theater, and they'll want George to provide a pleasant evening.

"George?" Lenny says. He looks down to the broken glass, shattered dishes, scattered pieces of crackly pizza bread, glistening with oil. George says nothing, seems to be in conference with himself. Kenny's up, wet, I see, from the spilled water. He's talking to George, but quietly, so I can't hear.

Then I see Wesley has left his backpack here. I dump its contents onto the table. There are paper clips, crumbs, a grimy permission slip, signed by George, for a class trip to the Cloisters. Ben says my name but I'm too busy digging; this is a *find*. There's a book, an actual book, not "text" arranged neutrally on some screen. As I pull it out I see it's *The Grapes of Wrath*, dog-eared, sticky, bearing Oprah's long-ago stamp.

"Is he reading this?" I ask.

"Yes," George says.

"So that would mean you're reading it with him?"

He doesn't answer. He turns away and goes to chat with the table of men in scarves, before I can talk to him, before I can say any of what I want to, and have to. I dig some more and find half a crumbled cookie. Ben is close to me, I see, with my coat, and Kenny is on the phone.

"Lola," says Ben, reaching for me.

I put Wesley's things, including the book and crumbled cookie, back where I found them. As Ben leads me out the night's music comes on, a lady pianist singing "I Happen to Like New York," my father's favorite song. As we go, we pass a group of six, coming in. I turn back, for just a moment, to see George come to greet them. If he sees me, he doesn't let on.

As we come outside Ben raises his hand and a cab pulls right up. Cabs are like dogs, Ben says. They either like you, or they don't, and they always seem to like him. He has his hand out for me but I need him, for a moment, before we get in. "What have I done?" I say. "How could I ever have done that?" He doesn't answer. We get in. As soon as we sit an ad comes on the tv for the Blue Man Group, the hundredth time I've seen it; the sound on the tv is broken, so in the back of the cab there's me, Ben, and the blue faces, looking at me, as if they knew what just happened. Ben turns the tv off, and we head west, with almost no traffic, not saying anything until we come to the light at the entrance to the park. It looks as if it's about to rain. I think of Wesley, out there in it, wherever he is, because of me. The light changes; we make the turn. "How could I ever even *believe* that? It's not possible. That's not me."

"What if it is, though?" He puts this to us both, as a biologist might ask a colleague after spotting a spark of something unexpected in a creature they thought they knew well.

"But I *always* know what I think," I say. "I have to; it *matters* to me. It's what civilized people do."

"They do a lot of things," he says. "Most of which, frankly, stink."

Traffic isn't moving. Ben pays the driver, and we get out to walk. Which we often do, across the park.

"But I'm bigger," I say, "than whoever that person who'd think that is, or say it."

"Don't be bigger. Please. The size you are is fine. Even if you're a hypocritical, racist homophobe, as has been fully proven today."

There are joggers, cops on horses, a woman talking on a cell phone as she pushes twins in a stroller. No one looks at me. Ben and I walk for a while, without talking. Then I stop; he walks on ahead a few steps. He stops, too, and turns back.

"I *did* that," I say. He doesn't ask me what. We walk on. "I always thought I was safe from that. I *assumed* it. That could never be me."

"Maybe," Ben says, "maybe we don't know who we are. Have you ever thought of that?"

"What do we do, then?"

We sit on a bench, both looking in front of us. At the other end, a runner stretches.

"I lied," I say, "about calling Theo."

"That was a good touch, though, about *The Wire*. You're good."

"Thanks." It's surprisingly warm; I almost don't need my coat. "What else don't we know about me?"

"A lot, probably. About me, too. I'll start a list."

"What do I say to George?"

"Come. Walk with me."

I do. I put my arm through his.

"I know one thing," he says. "I don't know if it will help."

"Tell me."

"That kid can be a real pain in the ass."

"That's no help, Ben," I say. "I knew that."

The rain never comes. We walk through the rest of the park, somehow seeing no one else, emerging on Fifth, setting out on the long, crosstown blocks to where we live, by the river, where we'll be, tonight, if he needs to come home.

9.

Wesley

Say I'm ten, or close to it. It was a Saturday, which was the day I'd spend partly with my dad, when he could. We went to the Museum of Natural History in the morning, where we saw the bird diorama I could never get tired of. And we saw rocks. I loved rocks. I could name a rock or mineral, no matter how small, from pretty far off. It was innate in me, I guess; I didn't question it.

So we left the museum, got on the bus, got off at Forty-seventh Street, and walked west a couple of blocks. We crossed Eighth Avenue and came to this little place called Ecco. As soon as we sat down guys came running from the kitchen with little plates of very good things. Then George came, also with plates, so the table was pretty much covered with them.

He sat down with us. I didn't know who he was. He seemed to know a lot about me, though, like he was a friend I didn't know I had. He asked questions that you'd have to know personal facts about me to ask. "So you guys tied, huh?" "Did you finish the *Harry Potter*?" And it wasn't just like he knew about me; it was like he was interested, too, in me as a person, and I was even less interesting then than I am now.

And I knew something—I just *knew*—that no one was telling me. It went like this. I had to pee. So I got up from the table and went down this hallway, one I've come to know well. I passed an open door, looked in, and there was George. Now, this was a long time ago; maybe the questions and little plates and George in his office were all spread out on different days and I'm adding them up as one. What matters is the room, George there, his saying, "Come on in."

He was at his desk. On the walls were a lot of signed pictures of laughing ladies, most of whom had big teeth in large mouths.

"Could I maybe ask you a question?" I said.

"Anything," said George.

"Who are all those ladies?"

"Actresses," George said. Those pictures are still up, and I'm even in one of them, now, with this lady named Chita Rivera (I think), who George brought me to meet one night when I was working. When he told her I'd been in *Bye Bye Birdie* (I was Hugo, eighth grade) she started to cry and George took our picture. As we both smiled she said, "Fuck Janet Leigh." Then she said, "Stay out of the business, kid." She was nice.

But back to then. "Thanks for all those plates," I said, on that day.

"Please," George said. "My pleasure. Did you like everything?"

"Pretty much. Yes. And about the *Harry Potter*?"

"Yes?"

"It was excellent, but disappointing, too," I said. He waited a while before he said anything else, like he was thinking about what I said, which was memorable because it didn't happen often then (or now.)

"God, I know just what you mean!" he said.

"Really?"

"I don't read a lot," he said then, amazing to me as no adult I knew had ever said anything like that before. "Would you recommend the book, even so?"

"It depends what grade you're in." I know I said this because George says I did. And I said something else, too, which George hasn't quoted back. "You love my dad," I said, and that was the thing I knew, the one that no one was telling me. I didn't use those words, maybe, but they're close enough.

"Yes," he said, on that day of the little plates. "Yes, I do."

Then I think I asked, "Does he love you?" Which would follow, and make sense. I don't remember. I could ask George. I went back to the table, and the plates kept coming, till it was time to take me home.

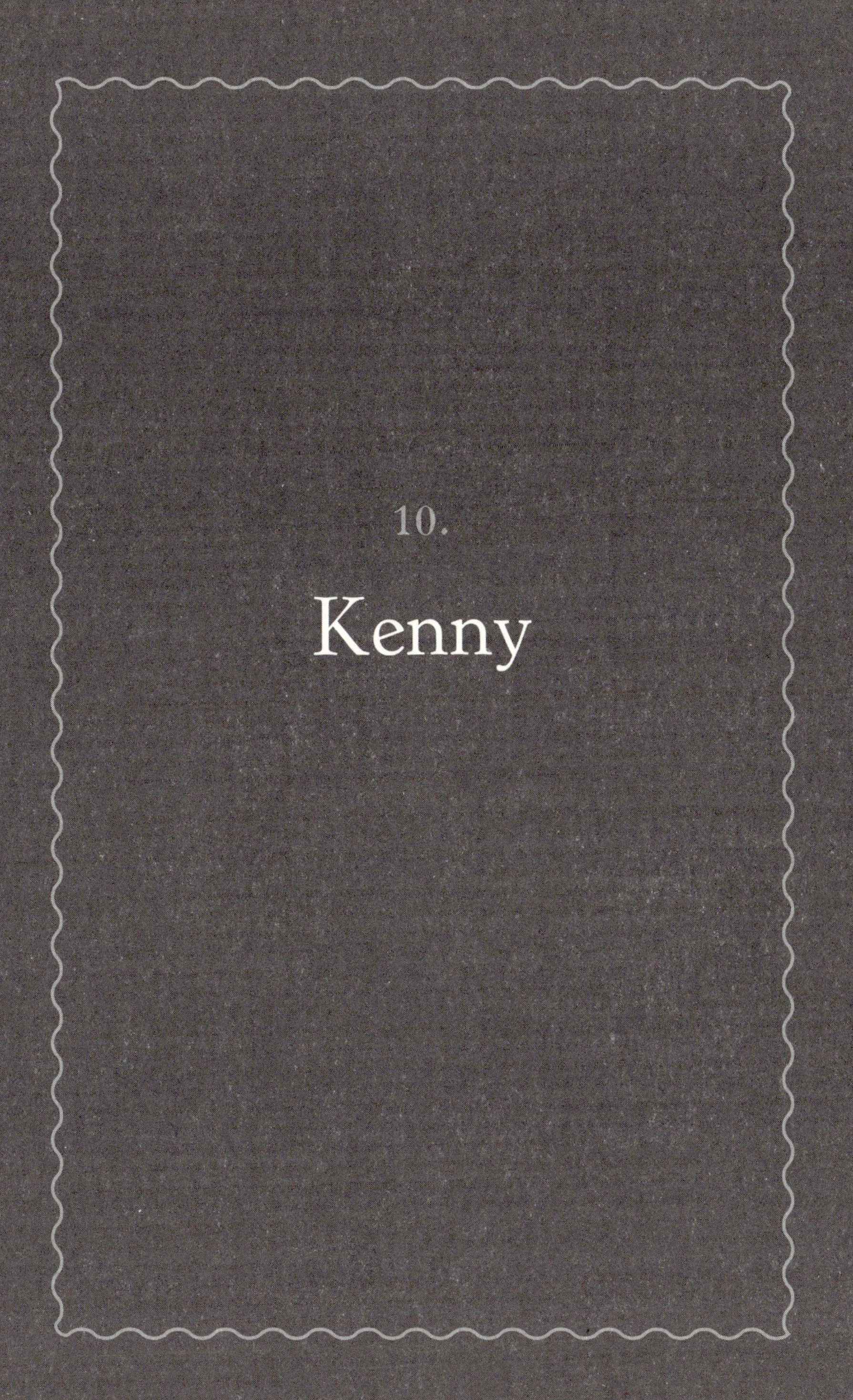

10.

Kenny

As I head east, they head west, people clutching tickets in their hands, hoping for something wonderful. I stop at a newsstand and load up on the holiday issues of food magazines, though we get them all; last year George did recipes from each of them. He was up for three days.

At Eighth Avenue I think, *Do we need milk?* People always need milk. Then I remember I never know what kind to buy. Two percent? Fourteen? George knows. I decide not to risk it.

As I let myself in I see flowers and wonder if they need changing. Again, that's George; he'd know. Even as I look at them petals start to fall. As I bend to gather them I see a slice of him, down the hall, on our bed.

"In here," he says.

So, with my magazines, that's where I go. The lights aren't on, but I can see he shares the bed with a pile of shoes, his and mine.

"Yes," he says. "These are shoes."

I don't know what to do. I want to be helpful and never know how to be. "Would you like me to put them back?"

He slips a shoe on each hand, pretends they're birds. "Shoes with wings on," he says. "That's the song. You always ask me what the song is." He sings, "*I've got shoes with wings on . . . Winter's gone, the spring's on . . . something doo-dah something . . .* Astaire, of course. Irving Berlin, maybe? Not sure. I'm a little drunk. Grappa. Want some?" He gets up, tries to squeeze by me as our bedroom's so small; George says the Dutch still own us, that we're squeezed together on a tight island, tight as Amsterdam houses. George says, George knows. "Excuse me. I want to go to the kitchen."

But I stay where I am. "I tried calling a few times. I went right to voice mail."

"That'll happen," he says. "Would you get out of the way?"

"Did she call here?"

"She's not going to call me, if she does. She's going to call you. Which I think would be better. And, if you really want to know, not that you asked, but the shoes are on the bed because it's dark in the closet and I don't mean that metaphorically. I can't see. So I don't know if there's a little missing shoe that needs half-soling. And it troubles me. So get the fuck out of my way."

I step back to let him pass, but he stays where he is. "What are those magazines?"

"Christmas issues," I say. "And maybe I shouldn't bring this up right now, but Charles and Margaret have asked us to the country."

"You go."

"It won't be the same."

"No," he says. He leaves the room, heads for the kitchen.

"I could try her again," I call out. He doesn't answer. "Because this isn't like Wesley, right?" Still nothing. "George?"

"Maybe it is," I hear him say. "Maybe you don't *know* what he's like."

There's a knock at the door. I feel dizzy suddenly; I sit on the bed. George comes out of the kitchen and undoes the lock, and I hear a Spanish-accented voice say, "From Lenny," and George say, "Thanks." I wait another moment, then go to the kitchen, where George lays out the good things Lenny has sent up. A cell phone rings. We have the same ring tones—programmed by George, "The Ballad of Sweeney Todd"—so it could be for either of us.

"Whose is that?" I say.

"Well, my guess would be yours, as yours is in your hand."

His phone now rings from the bedroom; as he brushes past me I see that I have two hundred and six messages. The most recent tells me that, yes, with his usual graciousness, Barney Frank has agreed to step in for me at Charlie Rose's table. *Yes, we have marriage equality now in New York. But remember, Charlie. There are fifty states.*

"That was Ben," I hear George say.

"And?"

"They haven't heard from him."

"Do you think I should I call Larry Frankel?" Larry, like many people we know, is a Surprising Gay Something, in his case a detective.

"Great idea," says George. "Unless I used those DNA samples as a marinade." Does he want me to laugh? I don't know. So I don't. "He's not a missing person, Kenny. He's missing on purpose. You just have to wait."

He goes back into the bedroom. From here, I can see the bathroom light go on. "Did you ever run away?" I say. I don't know why. I don't know if he's heard me. "George?"

Then there he is, with a stack of his framed actor pictures. They've been in our flaking bathroom since we moved in: George, young, being someone else, yet always also George, somehow.

"You're not going to throw those away."

"It's a little weird having them in there. I don't remember any of my lines. One, maybe. And you don't have to ask if I heard you. I did. And yes, I did run away, once."

"Great," I say. I just want him to tell me something, I just want to keep him here. "How old were you?"

"Thirteen?"

"That's young, isn't it?" I say, although I see this every day, hear all the stories, of the eleven-year-old gay kids who run, who don't come back, who can't.

"I didn't think so," George says. "I'd go to the public library, to read *Variety* every week, on a wooden stick. I'd go right to the theater pages, which they call 'Legit.' Which I thought, for a long time, was pronounced *legg*-it. I never heard it out loud, or any words I was interested in." I follow him back to the kitchen, where he picks a glistening mushroom from the salad but doesn't eat it, or offer it to me. "So I see in *Variety* there's an open call, for *1776*, for a tour. Anyone can walk in, audition. And there's a part for me, the Courier Boy. With a song. So I made a fife out of a paper-towel tube, and shoe buckles out of foil. And I packed a suitcase, because I was going to get it. There was no way I couldn't. I'd tell everyone I was an orphan, and when the tour was over I'd come back to New York and the Fosses would adopt me."

He stops, and even though I know the ending I want him to tell me more. "And?"

"What about you?"

I laugh. "What about me?"

"Your story. And don't say you don't have one. Everyone does."

"But I don't, George. I'm sorry. I just don't."

"Okay," he says, without quite saying it to *me*. He finds his wallet and keys, his coat, puts a scarf around his neck.

"Where you going?"

"Just out."

"But what if Lola calls? Or Wesley? Or he comes back? You have to be here."

He has the door open. So I'm going to be alone here; he might not come back. I let all that happen, downstairs. I didn't stop it. So he might not come back, and I won't know what to do, about anything. I don't *know* anything, and I never have.

And then, as the door opens wider, something rushes in, like a neighbor's scared cat, up and into my arms. *"George!"* I say. *"Wait!"* He understands, it seems; I don't know how. "I want to tell you something." I can't see his face. "Maybe it's not what you want to hear."

He's still turned away, looking out on the stairs. "Let's hear it," I think he says.

"It may not even have been running away. It couldn't have been more than an hour. And I knew I'd go back." He waits, doesn't tell me to stop. "We were in Yellowstone. I was with my family. And I was thirteen, like you were. I'm sure because my sister Alice had died that May. She was diagnosed with leukemia when I was ten."

"Okay," he says. "Alice."

"So it was the summer. Then, one day, it was the cocktail hour, and I excused myself to go to the outhouse." I see it, easily, a brown, painted cabin, as if I thought of it every day. "And there was a man."

"A stranger."

"Yes." I can see him, too. "Would you turn around? You don't have to, of course, but—"

He does, although the door stays open. "It was empty there, except for us. And he started talking to me as if he'd known me for a long time, like we were friends. And he said, 'I have a tent,' and I said, 'So do we.' "

George laughs, the first time I've heard it since what can't be just yesterday morning, since we were talking to Wesley.

"Do you want to know more?" I say. He does. "So I went with him, to the tent. He didn't molest me; I wanted to be there. I knew that. I came before he could even touch me. He asked if I could come again. I said, 'Thank you very much, but we're leaving tomorrow.' "

George laughs again. I get a text. My phone is in my hand; my phone *is* my hand. I look, to see if it's Lola. But it's just a reminder, from a proud and zealous gay website, that tomorrow is Cole Porter's birthday. I'm on a list. Yesterday was Halston, tomorrow Bessie Smith.

"Is there more? About the tent?"

"So after," I say, "I went back to my family. They didn't seem worried, especially. Maybe it was all only ten minutes. But I knew I needed a story, even though no one was asking for one. I said something like, 'Guess what happened.' Everyone looked at me. Then I said, 'I almost got trapped by a bear!' And that was it. They didn't ask for details. And maybe it's not much of a story but remember when Wesley asked us both, when we knew we were gay?"

"Yes," George says.

"I haven't thought about it, not since it happened. But I think that might have been it."

"In the tent."

"No. When I knew I needed a story."

Neither of us is interested in the food, but he cuts two small pieces of chicken, offering one to me.

"I never knew there was an Alice," he says.

"Really?" I say. But I'm sure he's right, though.

"I guess in ten years she's just never come up."

He turns away from me, washes his hands at the sink.

"It was a long time ago." What might he be thinking about me? What would *I* think? "I'm not good at things like that, telling stories about myself." I move closer. I want to see his face. "You are. I love that about you; everyone does. And you never repeat yourself—"

"Okay, then." He turns off the water, leaves the room.

"It was so long ago," I call after him. He doesn't answer. "George?"

"In the bedroom," I hear him say.

I go down the hall, past the framed costume designs, stopping at our doorway. He's in the bathroom; I don't wait for him to come out, I just start. "When I found out Wesley was hurt, on my way to the hospital, I thought to myself, *It's here. He's gay. I have a gay son now.* And he got it from me. I see that. That *thing*, to use his favorite word. And I thought, *No. I don't want that.* And I knew why, right away. Not because it can be hard, and I didn't want him to have to deal with that. But because *I* don't want a gay son. I want a straight one. They're better. Right?"

The bathroom light goes out. George emerges, still in his coat and scarf; he is ready to take off at any minute. The room is dark, except for light from the street. I wish I had a question to ask him, about where something is, or the name of a song I'm thinking of; he never doesn't know. I wish I could ask him what he thinks of me. "But there are still good things about me," I say. "You know there are."

I look to my palm, to my phone that's smart *and* worthy; it's all there. "Tomorrow, for example . . ." I tap the day, turn the phone to George so he can see there are no tricks, no secret compartments. I read. "Reminder . . . *Walt Whitman* . . . dinner, statue, overdue, shameful . . . Something has to go up *somewhere*, we're invisible in public spaces." I need my glasses now. "Also tomorrow, I give a speech at the Gay Legal Students Caucus—"

"You don't have to do this," George says.

But I do! "Saturday . . . right, the *New Yorker* festival. Me, Cynthia Nixon, Larry Kramer, Armistead Maupin, chatting with David Remnick himself. It's been sold out for months, can't miss that. Sunday morning, gay prisoners. Sunday brunch, gay *Afghanis.* Sunday night, transsexual potluck, and I'm not kidding. Sunday night . . . *True Blood. With G.* That's you. And it's got the gay subtext, so it's all right." I get a text. It's not Wesley or Lola. A group wants to honor me; am I available in April? "See?" I say to George, holding up my phone. "I'm a good man, in some ways."

"You're right," George says. "You are."

"But I'm not a good dad. Not for him. Don't tell me no, because I've seen that, every day he's been here with us. He came so he could get to know me better, right?"

"Yes. That was the idea."

"But no one asked *me*," I say. "Oh, maybe they did, as a formality. And what could I say but yes? Please, send him down, let him really get to know his gay dad. It'll be great! When what I should have said—" I stop. "I'm sorry."

"What were you going to say?"

"I don't want to tell you."

But I know that I have to, this thing that will "say" something terrible about me.

"Kenny," he says.

"I don't want to be known better," I say. "Which I should have said."

I see, on the bed, a few of his framed actor shots. There are the Toms, of course, Lancelot, Linus, Charlie in *Brigadoon*; every now and then he'll squeeze a pillow into bagpipes and sing "Come to Me, Bend to Me." The last time he did that we took it as a cue to turn off our phones, sleep our laptops, and spend a weekend in bed, three days still dirty enough, after ten years, to amaze us both. We watched the third season of *Battlestar Galactica*, all of it, assigning each other code names, like the characters in the show. I don't remember what they were. But George would.

"So are you surprised? At what I told you?"

"I don't think I am. No."

"Should we go away, possibly? Soon. For just a few days, nothing serious, when all this settles."

"'Settles'?"

"Wrong word, maybe. But the idea would be just easy, no airports. New England, say. See the leaves! And they're always good there on gay issues. Flinty individualism. Any state. Well, except Maine."

"Wow," George says, as if he'd just learned something surprising.

"What? Bad idea? There's other places."

"Oh, no," he says. "Leaves are fine. It's not that."

I wait. Let him take the time he needs. Because I need to hear from him what "it" is, because I don't know. "Then what is it, George?" He looks away from me when I ask this, shaking his head, his brow furrowed.

"I think it might just be this," he says at last, and as he does I think I know why I feel like this, unnerved. I don't think I've ever seen George struggle for something to say. "We don't know each other, Kenny. It's that."

"I thought we did."

He shakes his head.

"Are we in trouble?"

He doesn't say. But now, for the first time since all of this happened, I feel as if I know what to do.

"May I say something?"

"Of course."

"We haven't talked about what happened down there, this afternoon. About Lola, and her questions."

"Did I try to fuck Wesley, you mean."

"I suppose."

"What's to suppose? And I never got to answer!"

"You should never have been asked."

"Well, maybe you're right. You're the maven on this stuff."

"It just goes on, George. No matter how many gay weddings they go to, how many marvelous gay friends they have. Nothing changes! *People* don't! They just learn how to hide whatever it is they feel that makes them look bad for feeling it. This is what I *really* fight, every day. You have *no idea*."

"But I do," he says. "You're amazing."

"And I didn't stop her. I didn't stand up for you. I could have, I thoroughly see that. I don't know what happened. I don't know if you can ever forgive me."

"You seem to think I need that, to be stood up for. Defended. But I don't. And besides, she was—sort of right."

I laugh. Anyone would.

"Did I say something funny?"

"Well, you didn't say *that*."

"No?"

"You'd have to think she was right, and you don't. You can't."

"But I do."

"It's almost not worth talking about."

"Like Alice, you mean?"

"That's not fair," I say.

"It's not fair to be told what I think or don't think. Or *can't* think, even."

I'm so angry, or upset, or whatever this is, that I feel lightheaded. I push aside some of the shoes on the bed so I can sit. I need to be free from this for a moment, from the punches coming at *me*, Lola's little stings at me in the restaurant, George's coolly telling me things that could never be true as if they could be, as if they are.

And he has more. "Let me try to explain. I probably can't, I know that, it's not what I'm good at. But if you'll bear with me—" He makes a space for himself on the bed, next to me. For a few moments he says nothing. He smells like rosemary. A few moments more. I don't want to look at him, but I hear him whispering, sense his head nodding, as if in conversation, even hear what sounds like a short, private laugh. "Okay," he says then. "Whatever, but . . . she doesn't know me. Do you know what I mean?"

"No. Sorry. You're wrong! She *loves* you. Which makes it worse. Unless she's been pretending, which is entirely possible with people like Lola—"

He puts his hand on my arm, lightly, not to stop me but as if he is charging himself from me. I stop, anyway; I have an instant, inconvenient hard-on, like an eighth grade boy in math class as the end-of-period bell sounds. A few moments pass. Then he nods, giving himself some signal to move ahead.

"It's more like this, really. She knows me *partly.* How to say this . . . *downstairs.* Does that make any sense?" he says. Which Wesley says. He doesn't wait for me to tell him if it does or not. "I'm so visible, down there. I'm in my show." There's a burst of laughter coming from the street, from the well-fed and satisfied, leaving Ecco. "But up here, it's like she said. 'How do I know what goes on?' "

"She doesn't have to know anything," I say.

"Shut up." He takes his hand from my arm.

"I'm sorry."

"She knows me, down there. But up here, it's not the same. She hasn't got much imagination about it, but none of them do. They all know what they know already. Which is all they *have* to know because—*I* don't know—*because they all know it.* They know *I'm not safe.* That I'm two people. They may not be *aware* that they know it, but so what? They do! And *I* do. One me is the guy who remembers the names of your kids and your favorite pasta shape, who can rate and compare Elphabas. And the other one's the guy up here. The aging old chorus-boy queen—"

"Come on, George—"

"—alone with a teenaged boy, and we all know what that means. Which *she* knew, of course, but let herself not know. But now she has to know. And now all she's doing is her job. To keep him safe. Which he's not. No one is. But she still has to do it. We *all* have to do our jobs. So it would have been pointless for you to stand up for me. Sorry. Now, she's just doing her job. I don't hate her for that. I don't hate anyone who does their job." He gets up, looks down at me. "So there ya go, I guess."

I stay on the bed, watching as he goes out. Then I get up, follow, find him throwing away the flowers in the kitchen. "I was going to do that," I say.

"No worries."

"Where are those cigarettes?"

"What do you mean? We don't have any."

"What about that pack?"

He laughs, or that's what it sounds like. "Why do some people always think there's *that* pack? And that someone knows about it but won't tell. Do you know what I mean?"

What does *this* mean, I wonder, right now? That we're okay? "Well?"

"They're in here. To my left, behind *The Best of Gourmet, 1997*. I'll get them." He reaches for the book but stops just before he takes it down. "No," he says.

"But you said—"

He wipes crisp browned petals from the counter into his palm. "What do you want, Kenny?"

"A cigarette, like I just said."

"No." He shakes his head, so I try again.

"I want to call Lola. Maybe I'll get through this time. What if they know something?"

"That's not what I mean. What do you *want*. Not just in this minute, Kenny. We have to talk about this."

"You know what I want, George. I want us to be us, again."

"Which means?"

"You sound like Wesley," I say. "Which means, which means, which means."

"You *want us to be us again*. That's a little Marilyn and Alan Bergman–ish, isn't it? It sounds like something deep, but isn't, really?"

"I want to be how we were. Better? How about—how it was before he came."

"What else?"

"That's it. I do want that. I love you. You've got to know that. I'm sure you do." But he just looks down, shaking his head again, not even with me at the moment, I can tell, but with the ongoing conference inside him. "Is that not what I should want? Help me. It's ten years. Good things have happened, for both of us. We both know that. So what can I do?"

"I don't know."

"Then you want to leave, probably."

"I just said—"

But I say, "Wait." Because I hear him, for sure. He's above us, on the roof, where George hears him at night, and I don't. I look up. "That's him! Right?"

"Go, Kenny." He whispers, which we do now, with Wesley a wall away. *"Go up there."*

"Oh, come on!" I laugh as I think he's right; we *don't* know each other, at all, if he thinks I could do that.

"Why do you think he's here?"

"Not for me."

"Go."

"Well, I'm not going to, George." He says nothing. He's always saying *something*, except now, when I need it. I explain myself, as I see it clearly. "There's nothing I can do up there, you see. He knows that; he's not stupid. He's been here; he's *seen* me. He knows who I am." I want that to end it. And I want George to say something, to agree to that with me. As anyone would. But all he does is look at me. Why? "The one who should go is *you*. He'll be fine with you. *I* trust you with him." He doesn't go, though. I don't know what to do as I hear Wesley again, above us, moving around. And now as I look at George I see what might be tears. I've seen him cry many times, over television shows, a *cookie*, a fall day. But this is different;

I think he's crying for *me.* And he doesn't need to. I want him to know that, that I'll be all right. "I'm afraid, sweetie," I say. "That's all." He nods, and puts his hands on my arms. "I'm scared I'll disappoint him, and hurt him. He needs someone better than me. Someone like *you,* George. Okay?"

I don't feel right, suddenly. Nothing is where I remember it being a moment ago, as if walls have shifted, perspectives changed, things that a moment ago I could touch seem very far away. I won't say anything about it; he'll go up, and I'll go the living room and sit down until this passes. I move to do that, but he doesn't let me go. He tightens his grip on my arms, and as he does I lose my balance; the weight of each of us takes the other down. We're on the floor, tangled, holding each other tightly. I don't know what will happen if I stand up.

But then I'm all right. We both get up, both brush ourselves off, as if we'd just played together in piles of leaves. He doesn't hold me anymore. And we nod to each other.

"What should I do about tomorrow, do you think?" I ask.

"What's tomorrow?"

He knows. We talked about it. "Tennessee. The old man they kicked out of the nursing home when they found he was HIV-positive. He could keep his stuff there—"

"Right," he says. "His stuff, but not his 'person.' What was the term?"

He's asking *me* a question. This is new. Does it mean something good? "His *corporeal self* is the legal term," I say. "So, what do you think I should do?"

"What's it matter?"

"You're good at these things! Always. You always help me."

"You need to go. Which you don't need me to tell you."

"But I *do*," I say.

I see now he's kept on his coat (Barney's sale), and the scarf Ben and Lola brought him from Arrezzo. He opens the door, goes out without saying anything. He could be going anywhere, but after a moment I hear him on the first few steps to the roof. Then, nothing. *"I do need you, George!"* I say. Which is when a siren goes by, followed by a burst of Henry, two floors down, singing something about pretty women. Then, when it's quiet again, I hear what happens next, which is the door to the roof as it opens, although I don't hear it shut.

11.

Wesley

I see the Rosens in the hall. They don't see me. Theo thinks they have a certain ludicrous aspect, but he determined, with the help of a spreadsheet, that their ludicrousness only made up about twenty-one percent of their essential selves. He wanted to be accurate, and fair. It's good that they don't see me, as right now, even though they're turned away, I know they're both crying and both trying not to. Mr. Rosen holds Mrs. Rosen, and she holds him. I wonder did my dad and mom ever look like that, to the casual observer, who would know, like I do about the Rosens, that they're together. *There.* It's the word that comes to me. *There.*

Theo doesn't look good. Not that he should, as they're not letting him go home yet, or tomorrow, and maybe a day beyond that. He seems to be asleep and I don't want to wake him, but just as I'm about to go he opens his eyes like he's been waiting for me. He may be fucked up but he's still Theo, because while I'm deciding what to say he solves the problem for me.

"The cops were just here again," he says. "They want to talk to you some more, too."

"Okay, I guess."

"And they broke Fartemis. It turns out she's behind the unsolved murders in the American Girl Store. Which I knew."

I laugh, he sort of smiles, and I see this thing about him—a whole new thing—that I also see now isn't so new, that has always been there. *He likes it when I have a good time.* Even here.

"They were pretty nice, actually," he says. "They didn't do the Good Cop, Bad Cop thing, which was disappointing, in a way. Like whenever they do that on tv, I always think, I'd be on to them. I'd just laugh." His eyes close, for a moment, and I think, *Should I tiptoe out?* I start to, but then his eyes open again. "There's a bright side to all this, one might say," he says.

"Like what?"

"*Edge.* I mean like acquiring it. I do well in school. But that's not edge. I play lacrosse and soccer. That's not edge. I'm president of our class now—"

"And still no edge?"

"My college coach keeps going, 'Where's the edge? Brown likes fuckin' *edge*, Theo.' Now I've been gay-bashed. So?"

"Edge," I say.

"Providence, here I come." I see twelve individual lime Jell-Os stacked in a pyramid on his tray table. He picks up the one on top, hands it to me. "Have some," he says. "They keep bringing it. Maybe it makes you straight."

"I am straight."

"Well, you can always be straighter."

I eat the Jell-O; it makes me think of camp, and having colds, and is so good that I eat the next two on the pyramid right away, without asking. Before I reach for my fourth I tell Theo about everything that happened.

"You know what you should have told them?" he says. "When your mom asked if we were boyfriends?"

"What?"

"You should have said no. That we weren't. That we're just hooking up."

"At the Museum of American Folk Art."

"Excellent."

"She'd have been thrilled."

We both laugh at the same moment, and stop at the same moment, too. "So, how are you doing?" I say.

"Well, mostly I don't remember anything," he says. "I remember winning, pretty much, and Shannon's face when I made my speech, and thinking, So that's what it looks like when a face, literally, falls. And Fartemis's b.o., and most of Mr. Frechette's *pensées*." A *pensée* is a thought, in France; whenever Mr. Frechette makes one of his statements, the first thing he says is *"Pensée . . ."* "And as for the event? I don't question its reality—empirically, I mean—but mostly I don't remember it. Do you?"

I want to help him; I want him not to feel broken, or gay-bashed, or strange. I consider lying, but I know that he'd spot it, and no matter how fucked up his memory is now, he'd remember that; I know him. "Yes," I say, "I do. Is it weird not to remember?"

"They say it's normal. I said did that mean I wouldn't remember I was gay, either, but no one laughed or said anything. There isn't a Comedy Central wing or anything. So I've toned it down, because maybe they don't let you go home until you can prove to them that you're boring." His eyes close for a moment; he may have fallen asleep. "You can stay," he says, his eyes still closed. "I don't have a new daily Fact, though. Did we do flaying?"

"Yes," I say. "And I think we can probably skip today."

He opens his eyes. "May I perhaps offer you a lime Jell-O?"

"So, are you scared?" I say.

"About my head?"

"About going back to school."

"Yes," he says, at last, or what seems like that long. "You?"

"It's not school I'm scared of." I'm not fully sure what I mean by that, but he is, I can tell. So I know that he's still enough like himself to be himself; the guy, always, who gets it. "Where's your mom and dad?" I ask him.

"My dad went to get my computer. And my mom and Fartemis are getting me black-and-white cookies."

I wish he hadn't said this; it reminds me of how hungry I am. "I love those."

"We both do," Theo says. "That's something I remember. Maybe that's just there, permanently. Like other stuff. Like remember camp?"

"Of course," I say.

"I remember everything about that. All the teams, and the lanyard, and who seemed gay. Do you remember the Awesome Day?"

We both laugh; there's no way I could forget that.

"All those bluefish we caught," he says.

"Like nineteen."

"Dude! I'm Held for Observation Guy, and *I* know it was twenty-two! It *was*!"

It wasn't, but I let it be.

"I also remember," he says, or starts to say, because it seems like he's not going to say what it is. His eyes close again. "I'm okay," he says. "Don't worry."

"So you also remember—"

"Water."

"What about it?"

"How it tastes."

His eyes are still closed. "Wet, usually," I say.

But he doesn't laugh. I'm sorry I said it. "I mean how it tastes from a *stream*. From a tin cup."

I remember that, too, from camp. We loved camp. "A cup with pine needles stuck to it."

This causes him to open his eyes. "Water that you drink after you've been on a hike."

"And you're really thirsty."

"Fuck you," he says.

"Why?"

I see that he's crying. I wonder if he's been crying all along, behind his closed eyes. "*I* was going to say that."

"You still can," I say. But he doesn't. Tears stream down his face, but I don't mention them; some facts don't need talking about. This lady comes in to check on the Jell-O. Theo asks her to join us for one, but she tells us she just ate and the union probably would criticize her. She goes. Theo closes his eyes again, and I think maybe I should leave now. I start to tiptoe out, then I hear his voice.

"Hey, Wesley."

"Yeah?"

"You didn't have to do it," he says. "They wanted to get me, not you. You should have run."

"Yeah, right." I say. "I should have. Definitely. You're awesomely right."

"But you didn't."

"That was *irony*, Theo. Okay?"

"I know what irony is."

"I don't leave people who need me," I say, and as soon as I do I think: *Wow. I know something about myself now.* And I think, at the same time, *I have to get home. Somehow. I have to get home.*

He reads my mind, which reassures me that he's still himself. "So get started," he says.

And so I do.

12.

Ben

Professionally, at least, I'm a symbolic man, and only because of my field: eyes. If I was an ears, nose, and throat man I'd be, to quote my late Uncle Zell, just another Jew with a job. But that's not the case if you work with eyes in New York, or anywhere else, I guess. It goes back to Oedipus, probably, who had the bad judgment to blind himself. If I'd been there, then, with what we know now and if he hadn't eaten after midnight the night before, I might have been able to help a little. All right, a lot; I'm not a modest man. I know what I can do, and what I can't. And I find, although I try not to exploit it, that when people find out what I do their whole manner changes. Suddenly I'm a Someone, august, wise, Zagat-rated. This is mostly because, I think, everyone's afraid of going blind, except the blind themselves. They don't fear the going; they're already there. What does that mean? I don't know. I work with my hands, and from time to time like a piece of fish. Which Lola knows; she's become a fish expert, out of love for me. We even have a poacher, a gift from George. It fell off a truck, he said; we didn't ask questions.

"Ben?" She's in the kitchen, in the dark; she likes to cook in moonlight, like a witch. It helps her think, she says, and this is a lady who thinks all day. Which can cause problems for a person, but not her; like me, she's less smart every day, just one more reason why I love her.

"I'm here, my bride." She likes to be called that; it's the second or third time I've done it today, since we got home from the fun in the restaurant.

"Do you need anything?"

"I'm needless," I say. "I'm fine."

I join her in the dark, sneak my arms around her from behind as the water bubbling in the poacher sends up, in the steam, notes of salmon and dill. Saul Rapfkin, a colleague, is an oenophile who's always talking about notes; a finishing note of oak here, a sustained note of butter there; he's an idiot; we're all experts on the wrong things. And speaking of notes, I sing to Lola, quietly enough to still be a little bit musical, a favorite song of hers, ours: "Lost in the Stars."

"And we're lost out here in the stars . . ."

She joins me. *"Little stars . . ."*

"Big stars . . ."

"How can we be hungry, Ben?"

"I'm always hungry."

"I guess I mean me, then."

"You have to eat."

"Do I?" she says. "I don't know *what* I have to do, honestly. Because it seems, on the evidence of today, anyway, that I don't know who I am."

Does she want to know from me? Her back is still to me; I could ask her to turn, but do I need her face for an impossible enterprise?

Because how do you tell a woman in a kitchen the tale of her being and self, when she hates the Internet because it makes research too easy, helps others dig deep and deeper into who they are, when she's someone who can meet parts of herself she hates, as she did today, and still keep enough of the rest of herself in mind? She'll find out on her own, I'm sure of it; she's a brave girl; I am surrounded by brave people.

"Was that me today?" She turns to me now, and there's sufficient moonlight for me to see, easily, that she's been crying.

"She looked like you. She was an attractive lady."

"My God," she says. "How can you even look at me?"

"Easy," I say. "I like authentic people. I don't know why."

"How could I not know that I had that in myself?" she says. "How could I never have seen it? And what else is there that I don't know, or see? I accept *everything*, Ben! I make sure of that, to have problems with *nothing*. I'm a *New Yorker*."

"There are a lot of ways of being that, it seems."

"But this way? I can't believe that I let Wesley see that."

"What I think," I say, "is that you didn't have a choice."

"Well, I do now. But so does he. And I wouldn't blame him if he never forgives me. Not to mention George. Or even Kenny. I *don't* know what goes on; that's true. But where I went with that, and what was so—*easily there*. Where it had probably been all along. Which is what I hate the most. That it was in there all along. No wonder Wesley won't look at me. Why should he? He knows all he needs to know." She gently pokes at the fish. "It needs more time."

"I'm not going anywhere."

"God, I wish the Frick were open," she says. "It's okay, you can laugh. I know *what* I am. I just don't know who."

I see him now, getting off the elevator; I've left the door open, just in case. From the way he looks at me I sense he's not quite ready to be announced. I wave to him; he waves back. I don't tell Lola, though. Not yet.

"We can figure that out later, babe," I say. "I'll take Branwell out to pee. I'll be back."

Branwell hears this and is already at the door; he's gotten his own leash, as always, which has never impressed me; if he'd gotten his own breakfast, or tickets to a show, trust me; I'd acknowledge, and acknowledge, and acknowledge.

As I step into the hall and close the door he jumps on Wesley, slobbering, flinging gobs of it in the direction of Mrs. Lieber, widow, in 9-B. "Look at him," I say. "Like a cretin."

"What's that?"

The elevator comes; we get in. "It's the drooling," I say. "Which my mother would have said is *like a cretin.* A word that meant something once, but died. Or *passed,* as the ladies in my office say. Like you pass a test, or fail one. So does that suggest that death is a test now? Can you fail it? Can you retake it at a later date? Any thoughts?"

"I don't have any, at the moment," he says. "Would it be okay if I thought about it?"

"I'd be honored."

We sink, slowly, past floors of patrons, mavens, reservation-makers. He doesn't look at me, but that doesn't mean I can't look at him. So I do, and have thoughts. The first: Lola's right; in these two months, since he's been gone, his face has picked his father's to resemble. The second: this boy, bruised and hungry, running all over town, is engaged in the act of meeting himself, and will never be easy to fool.

The street, then; East End, the edge, the river right there. We walk a little, then cross for a look into Carl Schurz Park. I wonder if he remembers how I'd bring him here, as a kid, in his space suit; Lola's mother asked around this time what he wanted to be when he grew up, and he told her: *weightless.* Well, he's failed at that, fortunately.

"Does Mom know I'm here?"

"No."

Branwell looks up to him, then to me, then back to him. He settles his ass on the sidewalk, as much as telling us that he's not going to walk or pee until Wesley speaks. "Look," I say, "you can talk, or not. That's up to you. But I can't keep you out more than three minutes; she'd never forgive me. So I won't waste time asking if you're all right. You look terrible. But you looked terrible earlier. You don't look *more* terrible, though. That's positive."

He shrugs. "You can ask, if there's more you want to know."

"You're all right, then? Not that I'm asking."

He flushes, purple with grievance. "I'm *here,* aren't I?" He relents. "Sorry," he says.

"For?" I don't want to specify; I'm intrigued to hear him.

"For being that guy."

"Is this an Internet thing?"

He laughs; he actually laughs. "No! You know the Hall of Guys thing me and Theo have? That guy just then was Condescending Touchy Guy. They're *endemic,* one might say, especially at my school. And to answer your question: I'm okay. I guess."

"Is your dad aware of that?"

"No."

"Does he know where you are?"

"No."

"What about George?"

"What about him?"

"It seems to me he'd be just as concerned."

He laughs, with a laugh I hope he hasn't earned yet in life, one that sees people as disappointments, pretty much, others and oneself.

"I doubt that," he says.

"Why?"

He looks at me—straight at me, right in the eye—and laughs. "Are you serious?"

"Are you?"

"He hates me now. Wouldn't you?"

There's a bench, worn smooth by decades of widows and nannies; I sit, and wonder if he will, if he'll remember it was ours for years, for the half hour most nights before dinner. We'd come down, with some leaky dog or other, and discuss the details of our days; he never didn't trust me; I always felt honored by that.

"I think I probably wouldn't hate you," I say. "Maybe if you pushed and pushed and were even more obnoxious than you usually are. But even then, probably not. But that's just me."

"Well, I would," he says quietly. Then he settles, weightless, on the bench; if God was out, after a nice dinner, with His own old dog at the Eighty-sixth Street corner, I'd wave to Him, in thanks. We're under the eye of a streetlight; in his fatigue and lostness I see the ways in which he's still like a bird, really, species *Boy urbanis*; he's smaller at night, on a bench, resting from the hard work of being a hormone vat, a cell divider, a gatherer of evidence against us. A bird, exactly. Which means: careful; be a nest, not an answer; don't risk crushing the forming, mysterious bones.

"You want me to call them?" I say, after what I hope is a suitable silence.

He turns to me, with a golf-ball right eye and a black-and-blue left one. He wants me to help, and he wants me to leave it alone, too. "Can I think about that?" he says.

"Please," I say. "Cogitate. Hair won't grow on your palms, I promise. The night is ours."

"Yours, maybe." He gets up; I can tell he hurts. And I think, *He's responsible. He's learned that. He knows he exists in relation to others.* "We should go back," he says.

In the elevator we're silent again, both fixed on the square foot of air in front of us. As the doors open, Mrs. Lieber, stung by Madoff but with, luckily, as she says herself, "a smart Jew lawyer for a son," stands draped in her doorway, eating, as always, from a greasy bag of *rugelach*; whatever's in it must be working, as she's going to be ninety-three. I retrobarbically injected stem cells behind her maculae, which were dystrophic; it was a big success, which I mostly did for the cost of parts. As Lola says, she died two years ago but sees better than ever.

"So you're back," she says to Wesley. "We've missed you, in the elevator."

He doesn't say whether he's back or not. "Thank you, Mrs. Lieber. I've missed you, too." And he means it; he was right when he insisted in the restaurant that he's always himself; he is, poor kid. He is.

The old lady, sharp-eyed, extends the *rugelach* bag. "They're disappointing," she says, "but help yourself." He takes a couple, and she closes the door, choosing to forgo his pastry thoughts.

"Anyway," he says, his eye on our open door.

I say, "Anyway," too, but under my breath, to give him the space he needs. I don't have a claim, after all, or rights. He isn't real estate; he's a *boy*, and someone else's, even with the three thousand bowls of cereal I've seen him go through, the Great Lakes of juice, the apartment blocks of white boxes of We Deliver cold sesame noodles. But there are times, in the right light—so much, I've found, in my years with eyes, depends on the light—that he brings back pictures of my boy, David. Not the features, maybe, but the sense, of endlessly finding their way, choosing this, not choosing that, comparing maps of the forest; all ways seem equal until, one day, they're not. I must have been like that once, too. And now: here I am.

He bites his nails, which he never does. "You must be hungry," I say.

"Why do you say that?"

"Your nails. You're eating them. Like a first course."

"Really? I didn't even know." He puts his hands in his pockets. "Sorry."

"No worries," I say, which, like *passed,* is big with my office ladies.

He laughs when he hears this. "Mom totally hates that expression. She says things like that—really stupid, petty, tiny things—are the real marks of the end of Western civilization. Do you agree?"

"Jesus! You *listen*? I just say yes to her stuff like that. It's easier. She's not looking for a conversation." I look back, over my shoulder; Lola, still poaching in the dark, steps in and out of view, wearing, for some reason, a single heel. She seems to sense me; does she sense Wesley, too?

"Ben?" she says. "Would you call Kenny and George again?"

"Sure, babe."

"'Babe,'" Wesley says in a whisper.

"What about it?"

"Dad and George don't call each other anything. Or anything like that, anyway. Why do you think that is?"

He has more questions for me tonight than he has in years; I don't have answers for any of them, but I know, somehow, that it's all right. "Well, you're the one who's there," I say. "Do you have any thoughts?"

He says something, but so quietly I can't quite hear. I have a pretty good idea what it is, though, which makes me wonder if I should ask him to repeat it.

"It's nothing," he says, as if he knew this.

"Okay, then."

But it must not be, because he tells me now. "I said my thought was—it's *because* I'm there." He puts the uneaten *rugelach* in his pocket. "I should go in."

Something tells me to keep him there, for a final moment. "I've been thinking," I say; I haven't, but the lie buys me a moment.

"About?"

Now, fortunately, a face shows up, like an e-mail, its own story attached. "My first cousin. Sanford."

"The guy in Key West?"

"Very good. With the bed and breakfast. When he was Theo's age," I say, "he and my Aunt Frances would dress up, have tea, and listen to songs from *Kiss Me Kate.*"

"What's that?"

"It doesn't matter."

"I get told that a lot, it seems. All the time."

"The point is that we had euphemisms, then. Which is something you say rather than saying the thing itself, because it might fuck it up for people if you *said* the thing itself."

"I think I sort of knew that," he says—without snottiness, I might add. He's not perfect, God knows; he can chase you with pins, stick you to cardboard, tear off your wings with questions, questions, and more; we saw that symptom today, floridly. But is it masking a snottiness disorder? No. I'm eminent in diagnosis. That's not Wesley.

"And just maybe," I say, "in your generation—who are Martians to me, mostly, even you, sometimes—well, who knows? Maybe euphemisms will die off. Become unnecessary, that is. Like the golden toad. Or land lines. Or modern dance! And maybe, also—"

But he's got to be someplace, even though I can tell he's still sifting the possibilities. "You had a point," he says. "Not that I'm opposed to your thinking. Philosophically. Some of it's fairly elegant, one might say. But—"

"Here it is. My father, who appreciated language, took me aside once and said, 'Ben? Your cousin Sanford is a lovely, thoughtful boy. But he'll marry late.' "

"So that would be the euphemism, in this case. For gayness."

"A word we didn't even know," I say. "And now a boy can stand on a stage in school and make an announcement as to who he, fundamentally, essentially, *is*?"

"You're leaving out a part," he says. "The part where he gets the shit kicked out of him, too."

"Which is terrible. Which is because things happen slowly, in some species," I say. "In increments. With impediments. But they happen."

"That's what my dad says."

"Well, he knows a few things."

"Do you think David would have done what Theo did?"

I'm blinded, suddenly, by tears shoving their way, like New Yorkers, out of my eyes; I don't want him to see. "Who?" I say, although I know who.

He laughs. *"David."*

"Oh, that David. You mean my dead gay son." Of all the questions he's thrown at me tonight this is the one I can answer. "I do," I say, grateful he's asked me. "He was brave. Like your friend."

He seems satisfied with my answer. "Okay."

"And like your dad."

"I know he is," he says. "I know that."

"And like you."

"Me?" he says. "Why would you ever say that?"

I look back, through the partly open door, to my slice of Lola.

"I'm monopolizing," I say. "It's not fair."

"I should probably go in, right?"

A nest, I think; *not an answer.* "Up to you," I say, as my body moves, on its own, to a supper's aroma and the sight of my wife. "Up to you." I feel his hand on my arm then; it's been a long time since he's reached to me, for that, to keep me with him, to tell me one more interesting thing.

"Where do I go?" he asks in a near whisper. "Where do I go?"

Well, then! He's an audience plant, a ringer hired to make me, the Answer Man, look better than I am. I'm set, ready for words to pour from me like slobber from Branwell. "Well," I say. And what do I do but go blank! Words fail me, or I fail words; either way, one side's dead weight. But can I let him know that? I can't. I won't. *Dig, then.* Find *something.*

"Yes?"

"Tell me," I say. He nods, even though he put out the question, not me. "Do you need cab money?" Is this the best I can offer him? I was just about to be Shakespeare, or Shaw! And I remember, just after asking this, that the news hasn't broken yet; maybe he'll stay with us, where he can just walk through the door. And maybe he won't.

"No. I have a Metro Card. This is the last day, so I should use it."

"You sure? It would be a loan." I try to pass him a twenty, but no go; he's got squirrel hands tonight, closed tight around acorns. "You could work it off, like with your phone bill, with George. You can do a corneal implant for me. They're not hard." He reaches out; I think maybe he's going to take the cash! He floats his hand in front of him, as if trying to decide a course for it. But he doesn't turn it for a pouring of coins; instead he lets it float on its own until it rests, which is at a soft place on my shoulder.

"Hey, Ben?" he says.

"Yeah?"

"I'm glad Mom's got you."

"Yeah?" I'm a Beatle tonight, all I can say is *yeah, yeah, yeah.*

I turn back, look through the door, past our rooms of books and dog toys and gift boxes of macaroons from Paris until I see her, my girl, glowing like just-found *afikomen*. She'll be wondering where I am. Supper's more than ready, surely; there will be enough for all if he wants to stay.

"What can I tell you?" I say. "I'm putty; I'm hypnotized. And on top of that, she sees perfectly." She calls for me. Does she know he's here? "Coming, babe," I say. But it seems I have one more thing for the two of us, out here. "And the thing is, Wesley—"

"Yeah?" he says, which I'm grateful for; I have too many things to say; like him, I have to choose one, at least for now.

"The thing is—I cherish her."

"'Cherish,'" he says, cocking his head like Branwell does, or used to, when he still felt he had to woo us. "What do you mean by that, exactly?"

I'm not an eloquent man; I'm about seeing, not saying. But

I'll try; I will always try. "Exactly? It's *in*exact, probably, if it's anything."

"Inexactly, then."

"It's like love," I say. "It's something like that."

"How?"

"It's *related* to it. That's more what I mean."

"Oh."

Maybe he'd be satisfied at this point, happy with my answer to his question. But I'm not; I see a little more. "That *grows* from it."

"From love."

Has he been in love? We don't know. Will he be able to love? Oh, yes.

"And maybe it's even a *place*," I say. "That you get to. Or maybe it's none of those things."

"Oh, no," he says. "I doubt that." Then: "Wow."

"For what?"

"Everything. This has been an awesome day. Can I say *awesome*?"

"This once."

"And this *cherishing* thing, Ben," he says. "Do you think it's better than love?"

"You'll find out, I think," I say. "In fact, I'm sure of it."

"I will? Where?"

"It's different for everyone, probably. Maybe it's somewhere in *The Grapes of Wrath*."

He groans. "I doubt that."

"Me, too."

I'm sneaky, now; I stuff my twenty into his pocket. Before he can protest the elevator comes, as if we'd rung for it; he now has two open, waiting doors. Isn't there usually a third, in the fables? Maybe not, when the two you have already both might have tigers inside. He looks from one open door to the other, and does it again, and once more. Then, without a good-bye, he steps into the elevator, to turn the page to the next chapter of his night.

13.

George, Wesley

He has, as it happens, taken the train, anyway; not to pocket Ben's twenty but because trains, all day, have been willing to carry him and have helped, in their subtle directive sway, in his decisions where to go. He's grateful to the train, then, and sees it as a tame beast, with a soul; he is, after all, a city boy. And, also, as Theo once said, does anything really significant ever happen in a cab? Taxis, unlike trains, just aren't all that interested in you. On the subway he says some of this out loud, loud enough so he can hear it but not for others to hear, too. Because suddenly, he's finding, everything is practice, for conversations that haven't happened yet, with people he's yet to meet. And as for the cash from Ben? He'd never take it back, of course, so he has decided to give it to George, as the last payment on his phone bill. That's if George doesn't hate him, naturally, as he is likely to do. If he doesn't, George will want to let the balance go. But the boy won't go for that; what kind of man makes a deal and then, at the end, suggests he never took it seriously? No kind. Period.

It is eleven, or around that. He doesn't have a watch; like everyone all over he wants his phone to do the work of twelve magic oxen, machine division, and he doesn't have his phone. He gets off at Fiftieth, walks down three blocks, then turns west with the flow of traffic. This is Forty-seventh, a street he knows mostly in the mornings, when it steams and simmers sweetly, like something waiting to be eaten, dunked into coffee, shedding delicious crumbs. He works against the crowds, disappointed or delighted, coming out of theaters to either go home or to one of the hundred restaurants like Ecco, for a bite, for a salad with *soppresatta* or garbanzos. As he's a stupid kid, occasionally, he doesn't think that *he's* hungry, which he should be, but that he's invisible, instead, which is stupider yet; he with the puffed, meaty face, the stitches and swollen lip, the taste of blood still in his mouth. Who would notice a boy like that? Then he hears his name! It has to be his, because how many people are saddled with it, really? The callers turn out to be those old-lady Galligan girls—the twins—at their ninety-four-degree angles to the pavement, making their maidenly way home from ushering a night's performance. He offers them each an arm; the sisters try to decline, for their own reasons, but he insists. His gallantry might be unnecessary, as they have a mere half block to travel. But Wesley, who remembers, more or less, everything interesting or funny that has ever been said to him, thinks of what George told him about their breakability. So he will not be the one to let them fall, and crack, and shatter; sorry. Not he.

"Take this," says Mary Galligan, who is now at a hundred and five degrees, as opposed to the ninety-four of her sister, Therese. She has plucked a powdery dollar from her pocket and, with her toy hands, presses it upon him.

"Take this," says Therese, offering her own dollar, this one with a half-sucked Life Saver stuck to it.

He's caught, then; this is the third time tonight he has been offered cash. Will the ladies be as sneaky as Ben, and stuff singles in his pocket? But he decides not to resist; he understands tonight, as he might not have before, that to accept what someone wants to give you is, in its way, a kind of bravery. The next assist to the Galligans, he decides, should there be one, will be free.

"For college," says Therese, about her dollar.

"A girl," says Mary, about hers.

He nods to both suggestions, and hopes someday that, when people think of him, their imagining of the poles of his life will be—what?—broader, say.

He sees the ladies to their third-floor rooms. But they're not done with him; Mary, or Therese, hurries in and returns with a package of shortbread. She hands it to him, then, whispering, vanishes behind the door with her twin. He opens the package, eats a cookie; it is the only thing he remembers eating since a bite of pizza bread yesterday afternoon, if that was, indeed, yesterday afternoon; he's sure of very little, right now, mostly the avenues he's suspended between (Eighth and Ninth, each with its own views as to how traffic should flow), the cookie in his mouth, its grit dissolving into sweetness, his own skin and hair and rollicking, restless cells.

He is sure, too, that he has more stairs to climb, even if he's unsure what to do when he gets there. *Maybe it's somewhere in* The Grapes of Wrath, Ben said. Which reminds him: he's now even more behind than he was and, whether he's welcome or not, he somehow must get his backpack as the book is in that. So, like a cat, he gets to four and then, hesitating two steps below the landing, he becomes Superman, or at least acquires X-ray vision skills which, if he also does well on the SATs, might help get him into Brown. He can see through the door he helped George scrape and repaint (from shit brown to what George calls Della Robbia blue) to the stack of Playbills on the kitchen table, to George's shelf of tinted French salts, even to the two men—George and his father—talking to each other, a sound that causes him to head, for now, to the roof. He likes it there; he has come to think of it as his, even though it isn't, of course. Still, in the time they've let him live here, it has been the one place he can go where there are no college coaches, papers due, adult brows that wrinkle and say, without need of words, that they are worried, even sure, that you will amount to nothing.

When he steps out onto the tar-paper roof what he sees, first, is a book. Whose could it be? Not his, he knows that; he comes up here, yes, but late, to think and to walk; never, certainly, to read. The book is a paperback, its title *The Secret History of the Pentagon Papers as Reported in the New York Times.* He opens it; at each of a dozen paper-clipped markers someone has written *Song*. The copyright date is 1971. His dad and mom were three, Ben was twenty, George had not yet been born. Which of them could he ask about it? There is too much he doesn't know. His mother and father would, first, wonder why he's asking; is there significance to his question, or something they should worry about, without saying what that something is? They would then go on to be worthy, and stern; he knows this isn't fair, but he's too weary, right now, for balance. Ben, he knows, would make him laugh; he would like to be as funny as Ben is someday, funny in that way that doesn't separate it from the rest of life. And George would plead ignorance, as he always does; when Wesley asked him, not long ago, if he could shed any light on the Oslo Accords, George said, "It's my blue pantsuit, right? You're thinking I'm Hillary Clinton."

This is when George appears, at the open door. He has heard Wesley on the roof, as he always does; he thinks, first, that Lola should be informed of his whereabouts, if she doesn't already know; it is as much a habit for him to be *seen* as trustworthy as to *be* trustworthy; one is always in need of a defense. But that's different now, or, at least, changed. He has been accused; he has not been defended; he had forgotten how unsafe it always is. But he remembers now. So should the two of them be up here, alone? Best to stay at the doorway, then; best to not step through. But then? He wants to know if the kid is all right, this boy who, through an instinctive show of courage on a friend's behalf, has changed everything for everyone. How will my life change? George wonders. He understands Wesley's nights up here now; a roof is a good place to go when you can't imagine what will happen to you.

He waits; if Wesley is aware that, even tentatively, George has joined him, he doesn't let on; he is turned away, looking through a book; he is posing, with thoughtfully furrowed brow and a boy's ever-broadening shoulders, for a picture whose title anyone could guess: *Boy, Reading.* George sees the moon, light-years closer up here than it is four floors down, on the street. He thinks of the words *a little silver slipper of a moon*, and, for a moment, can't name their source. Then it comes to him. Of course; Tom in *The Glass Menagerie*, writing poems on the lids of shoe boxes; the remembered words are said by his mother to him, when she asks him what he wishes for and he tells her, of course, it's a secret. His nose finds work, now, as the street's cuisines compete for customers. Southern Italy. Northern. Sicily. Crete. You might think, up here, that the whole city had been breaded and fried, with rivers of *sauce diavolo* running through the oil-absorbent streets. George has taught Wesley tricks with calamari, zucchini rounds, stubby pencils of polenta; he's got a light touch with a fryer, which isn't something you can learn. Will he remember this skill? Will it help him, in life, at all?

"Hey," George says, quietly enough that the sound might have come from an open window, or someone's tv. Wesley hears him, but he doesn't turn or look up from his book. The *Pentagon Papers*, which he'd not heard of as of four minutes ago, has become all that matters in the world, somehow. He even moves his head, side to side, like an old typewriter carriage. He's never seen one, but George has, of course, and it's what George thinks of as he watches. He also thinks of acting, actors, all the classes he took. As he gazes at Wesley from the doorway he decides Wesley is "indicating," which is the worst thing anyone can ever say about an actor, at least as an actor sees it. This means that he is *performing* something instead of being it; it is, for an actor, the way of the coward. But the kid isn't either, George thinks, an actor or a coward.

"We heard you," George says.

Wesley turns a page, nods to himself as if it is all coming clear to him. He wants to look back, but for what? What would he say? He doesn't want George to go, but he doesn't know how, when the time comes, he'll be able to turn to see him.

George seems to understand. "In other words," he says, "you've been heard. Okay?" And is this it? He doesn't expect an answer, knows he has no right to say more; the boy is someone else's. But he can't help himself; he has a final word left that wants out, wants to take the air. It's a name. That's all. "Wesley," says George. Wesley gives no response, other than turning a page. Below, on the street, someone opens the restaurant door. George hears a chorus of "Happy Birthday" from within; Lenny will be doing what he, George, usually does, lighting the candle stuck into the birthday person's *torta della nonna*, joining in the song to end, as he has so many times, the big night out of a table full of strangers. Maybe, he thinks, he'll stick his head in down there. There are always people to greet, with whom he can be knowing, whom he can reliably delight, who come for a dose of the small bright gifts he has and likes to give. He's already a few steps down when Wesley clears his throat.

"I hear you," says Wesley. "Okay?" This said, too, without looking at him, at George.

"Okay," George says. Question, answer, simple as that, nothing guaranteed beyond it. George realizes, though, looking at his back, that he made a promise to him, lost in the events of the last thirty-six hours, to consider and answer a question, a promise he has yet to fulfill. But he says to himself: *Wait. Don't breathe. If you breathe, it breaks.* "In case you're interested, not that it's that interesting," he says now, "but there's some lemon almond polenta cake downstairs. You usually like that." Because Wesley is still turned away George can't see his mouth move, as the pleasure center in his brain kicks in, going back, Wesley thinks, to the time in race memory when man first walked upright and first had friends over, for some grass tea and a little lemon almond polenta cake; he wants to get into this with Theo, soon, when some of this present shit clears and they can get back to their Facts and Interesting Things. Until then, he'd love some of this cake. But he overrides the instinct, and stays turned away.

"No, thanks."

But George remains, his host's instincts flowering; Wesley is a customer, he decides, a guest, come in because he's heard good things from impossible-to-please friends. "And there's spinach lasagna," he says, knowing Wesley loves it and hoping he's telling the truth, just in case Wesley should spin around, light up, say he wants some. "With chanterelles—"

"That make people fall in love with you," says Wesley, without turning, and startling George. "At first sight."

"What?"

He sighs. "You *said* that. This morning. Or yesterday morning. Or whenever it was." He turns now. "Don't you remember?"

"Of course I do. And I meant the organic ones, by the way."

Wesley doesn't look away, but he also doesn't laugh. And George wishes he hadn't said it, wonders if he *wanted* to crack the kid up, even though Wesley is hardly the Sammy/Liza spit-take type. He is, in fact, pretty stone-faced; George thinks back to the two months of mornings in the kitchen, the talks downstairs, all the times George has joined him, in grabbed moments, at the small back table in the restaurant where he has done his homework over a bowl of *pasta alla Norma.* If there was laughter, it was usually from something Wesley said to *him;* never has he sought to be charmed, or *hosted.* Henry, on the second floor, opens his window and, accompanying himself on the piano, sings a little Sondheim, as he does all day. *Pack up the luggage . . . la la* LAAA *. . . Unpack the luggage la la* LAAA . . . George thinks that the ideal location for this song to be performed would be at airports, at security lines. And, just as he thinks this, and wraps it and tucks it away, to be used later, he also thinks: *Oh, yes, I'm delightful. Even after a day like this; it's money to me. And this boy came back here, for something, tonight, and that's not it; he's not here to be delighted. And that's all I know how to do.*

"Let me give you something," George says. "Anything."

Wesley looks, quickly, at him; some might read what's come to his face, in a flush, as puzzlement. But not George; he reads what he has never read there before, which is disgust. "Why would you want to do that?"

"Because I'm good at it. I know what to do."

Wesley turns away again. George wishes he had some magic, mushrooms, anything, to call him back. As he looks around, references to rooftops flood his mind. Brando and the pigeon coop, of course, in *On the Waterfront*, a film he shared with Wesley. A thousand terrible romantic comedies, where He wins She by surprising her with champagne and candles and what is always, George knows as a professional, a most impractical *al fresco* meal. And the Hunchback, on his roof, pouring hot lead on the mob come to tear him from his bells. *I should try that sometime*, George thinks. *Yes; pour lead on Hal Prince; ring bells; cackle*. He could go on, but he stops himself there; he is, as always, a little ashamed of what he knows. *Oh, I am trivial*, he thinks; *my thoughts aren't those of a serious person, of any kind of man.*

"It would just be plain lasagna," George says. "There wouldn't be chanterelles, so there's no risk of magic. The guy at the Green Market was sold out by the time I got there yesterday. "

"Hey, George?" Wesley says. "I don't want lasagna, or polenta, or anything *delicious*. I just want to be left alone. Okay?"

"Okay."

"I'll be gone soon."

"Do you need anything?"

"I already told you no."

"You left your backpack."

"Oh, I need that," says the boy.

"You left it in the restaurant and I took it up with me."

"Why did you do that? If you'd left it downstairs, I could just go get it. And Dad's there, right? I know he is. I heard him, talking to you. I wasn't eavesdropping."

"I wouldn't have thought you were," George says. "You're not like that."

"No, I'm not," says Wesley, slightly astonished and a little angry, as one is when a quality one knows one possesses is, finally, acknowledged by someone else.

"So do you want to go get it?" George asks. He must ask this; he knows that. He knows that every moment up here is one that greatly counts. So he hopes that Wesley's answer will be no; he does not want to lose him now, before he has kept his question-answering promise, even though he has no idea what his answer might be. Does he even have an answer? And if he does, is it the right one? He has always been cautious, aware of the world as a vast map of wrong steps, and watchful never to take one; he has made a living out of his learned skill of intuiting what would please others and leading them to it.

"I don't think so," Wesley says.

"Well," George says, "that's understandable."

"Why?"

"I don't know."

"And I think what I *really* want is to be alone. Up here. Not to be rude, or anything."

"Well, that's understandable, too," George says. "You've been through a lot. And you're not being rude."

"Dad would see it differently. He said, 'You've really gotten awfully rude.' You heard him. You were there—"

"But I don't agree. Because I don't think that's who you are."

"You don't know who I am!"

What George does know, as Wesley's feelings scribble themselves across his face, is that he's got him now; he's his, for the moment, and however long he can make it last. "I'm sure you're right. I'm sorry."

"You are?" Wesley says. He is so startled to hear this he comes close to asking George to say it again. *I'm sorry*; none of his Olders (which is what he and Theo call them) have ever said those words to him. And why would they? They're magazines, about themselves. They dispense opinions with the gravity of Justices at the Highest Possible Court. The words *I'm sorry* tend not to fly from the mouths of such people; such solid citizens; such New Yorkers. No.

"I am," George says.

"Well, like I said, I just want to be here alone."

"Sure."

"Thank you."

He is never this crisp, George thinks. He is never crisp at all. He has agreed to leave, but he isn't going to, not yet. He has a promise to keep; Wesley might have forgotten about it, but he hasn't. "What's the book?"

Wesley sighs, with a rear mezzanine–pitched largeness; he has learned, George can see, to be a bit theatrical in the time that he's been here. *Has he picked that up from me?* he wonders. He was always told he was that way by his father, and not as a father might note in a son an admirable trait or the promising glimmer of a future career path. So he has always tried not to be—theatrical, that is—even though he went into the theater. "Just a book," Wesley says. "So did Mom call here?"

"No."

"Really?"

George doesn't say yes or no. Wesley is looking at him now. The reading display is over. He closes the book, puts it on the ledge, aligns it neatly. "And the book," he says, "is about this thing called the *Pentagon Papers*. Do you know what that is?"

He doesn't. He should, of course. *Pentagon*; a serious word. "Ah," says George, "that must be Henry's. He's been writing a musical based on that."

"That makes sense, then. He's written the word *Song* all through it."

"I think he's on to something. Lenny thinks it's a terrible idea. He says the next thing you know, someone will want to write a musical based on *Pygmalion*."

"What?"

Once again, out here, in this place that, for George, feels a little too much like a stage; this seems to be the place to regret things, for George does regret what he's just said. He used to enjoy Wesley's puzzlement, not because it made him feel superior but because he so enjoyed filling him in, giving him something, useless, probably, in his life, but something of his, nonetheless, like encoding some minor entertaining gene that might, years later, provide him some mysterious joy in the world. But that's not how he feels tonight. "I'm sorry," he says, a different kind of sorry this time.

"Why?"

"I say too much, sometimes."

"You do," says Wesley. "Sometimes."

George sees what it has taken for Wesley to do this, to agree with George's own self-criticism but, at the same time, to not to make it *larger*, turn it into a condemnation; to let it stand. "I know that. Believe me."

"But just sometimes." George knows that Wesley hasn't said this to make him feel good, or better, but because it is, genuinely, how it seems to him. Wesley, George sees, has added him up, or started to. "But like I said."

"You just want to be alone."

"Thank you," Wesley says, and George thinks this is the second time tonight that he has been thanked by a Bowman. Wesley turns away again, but this time he doesn't bother to pretend he's reading. Again, George could leave him here; he probably should, he thinks. Then again: or not. And he doesn't, in fact, know which of those choices he's made until a moment after he's made it. And then, there it is.

"The thing is—" George says.

"George—"

"I owe you."

"What are you talking about?" says Wesley. He's even laughing, a little. "What could *you* possibly owe *me*?"

George understands, he just does, why Wesley has just stressed the words—*you, me*—and doubts he could have meant for George to hear them in any cruel way. But they have an effect; they bring him back to what he has been asking himself, again and again, since yesterday: *Who am I to this boy?* In Wesley's time here, with him and Kenny, that has never come up; the question would seem to have stepped out, with white-gloved jazz hands, from the darkness. But as Lenny said last night, when George came straight to work from the hospital and had to, in a flash, delight the room, how can the coming of that question have been a surprise? So there the question is. He came up with part of an answer, on his own, when trying to describe himself at the ER: *There's no name for me.* And then the rest of that answer, the part with weight, evident instantly to others and so clear it hardly needs to be said: *Nobody. I'm no one.* But even with that, he still made a promise, and he is going to keep it. He doesn't know how, but he will still try. Which involves starting somewhere; somewhere, wherever *you* decide it is, is always next to somewhere else. Which is where the map begins.

Start, then; something. "I can't answer that, Wes."

Wesley, again theatrically, shudders a little. "I hate my name."

But George isn't here to tell this kid he *should, shouldn't,* not about anything. *Don't think,* he tells himself; good advice, from acting school. But he is not acting now. "There are a lot of questions I can't answer," he says.

These words explode Wesley. "That's fine!" he cries. "That's totally okay with me! So I can go now, because believe me, I don't *want* to be here. I made a promise to Theo, but he can call you himself."

George ignores this. "Yesterday morning you asked your dad and me some questions. He answered. I didn't. And as I remember it—which I should, I was there!—I asked for time. I don't need any more time. Time's up."

Wesley stands now, or, that is, his body does, as it seems to have acted without his agreement or knowledge; he's a puppet, pulled from its peg, limbs flopping and unfolding, heading in nine directions at once. "It doesn't matter about time. You don't owe me anything, George. You're just my dad's boyfriend. Okay?"

This doesn't sting, which surprises George. And what surprises him, also, is that he hears the words but, at the same time, hears a voice dubbed over, giving the real meaning: *Stay. I will. Even if it's just a moment more.*

"Okay," George says.

"Okay?"

George has startled Wesley again, as he did when he said he was sorry. "That's right."

"So you should go, then," Wesley says.

"Because you 'just' want to be alone."

"Right."

"But you also don't want to be here, if I heard you correctly. So which is it?"

"I don't have to tell you!" Wesley says. But George knows he wants to, or wishes he could. "So please: *just go.*"

"You can really be a brat, can't you?"

A third surprise, now, for Wesley, possibly the biggest yet. He doesn't disagree, and he's grateful to have it pointed out like this; it's specific, and real, and it gives him the choice to be aware of it, to do something about it. "I can?" he says.

"And I'm thinking that maybe the one who should stay here is—" A little moment makes itself, on its own, a pause to be filled; George hasn't been behind it. "Me. So why don't *you* go?" As he says this, and takes in Wesley's astonishment, he feels a shift in his center, a weakness in his knees, as if the roof was the deck of a ship, in a storm, listing. Will it tip him off, to send him floating down, like the *Angels* angel, to the street below? *Greetings, Prophet!* Thud. He was good in *Angels,* in the way you are when you know you are, which might not be that good, in the end. "Well?"

Wesley's bruises glow; his stitches swell; his eye looks as if it might pop its socket. "Well, what?"

"So," George says, bowing to what he sees approaching him or, better, maybe, the vehicle he finds himself on. "So I'd take the train."

"The *train*?" Wesley gets up, and he feels it, too, the same odd listing of the roof. "George? I'm going?" he says; he doesn't know where. "And I really sort of need my backpack?" He hears himself, how his voice shimmies up the ropes of question marks, which he usually makes sure it never does; he and Theo regard this as a sign of idiocy, even though most of their teachers do it now, too, as if embarrassed by the smallness, the rusted, dead information they are still obliged to impart. "All my Innocence stuff is in it, and *The Grapes of Wrath*, and part of a sandwich, and some *change*. I need that stuff. I can come for it tomorrow, if you'll bring it down to the restaurant—"

"Listen to me," George says. *"This matters."* He has never said that to anyone before, and he's not sure why he's said it now; the words crack and spark around him, like a sweater too long in the dryer. He's unsure what, if anything, will follow; all he's got is a train, the train he'd take to the city (thirty-six minutes; never more, never less) on occasional Wednesdays, when he would slip, thrillingly and for free, into the first half hour of a matinee's second act, at risk every moment of being caught, which never happened, but always could, which was what made it worth the risk. And then there was the thrill of wondering if he'd make it back to the train to be home in time to tell his equally thrilling Wednesday lie. Wesley, in his months of Mondays-through-Thursdays, has taken pleasure in hearing George's (carefully edited) history, but George has only brought out the goodies from Volume II, the hundred and one tales that begin with the time of the tours, the Toms; the tales that reliably *delight*; George is such *fun* in them; George is so *George*. And those tales don't matter.

This does; this matters.

"George—" Wesley says, trying to step around him, to leave the roof. He stumbles; George catches him, easily, like an envelope dropped from a window into his street-level waiting arms; Wesley's frame feels perfect and tiny, like a squab's. For a moment George has him dipped in his arms, like a lover or, at the least, a tango dancer. He hoists Wesley up, settles and balances him, lets him go.

"You okay?"

"I'm *fine*," Wesley says. "You *caught* me."

George notices that Wesley is just about eye to eye with him; when did that happen? Since they've been up here, tonight? "That's right," he says.

"So would you let me pass, *please*?"

He starts to swing around George, but George, with just a quick touch of his finger to his sleeve, stops him; even as he does, even as the small *zap!* happens and has its effect, he hears voices, in chorus, calling out the same familiar whispered warnings, from open windows, all around the town: *Do not touch, restrain, instruct, go near.* He has always obeyed.

But he doesn't now; he presses on. "I'd take the train," he says, "and I'd come into the city. Cutting school, of course. Every couple of weeks; I couldn't do it too often."

"You're hurting me," says Wesley, but he does nothing to set himself free. He has never seen George like this, or any adult in his life, for that matter; one gone *wordless*, applying to him for patience, letting him know he has value as a *listener*, not simply as someone *expected* to listen and, quickly, start the journey to be a Better Person.

And George sees a picture, taken on this train. The aisles are wet, from tracked-in snow; no one knows, as the train works its way through the Long Island towns, that the snow will continue, through the day, the state, through most of the night to land, triumphantly, in the record books. On the train a man and a boy sit facing each other, their knees almost touching. The man, George knows, even as he's pictured from behind, is himself, as he is now, pretty much, maybe less tired-looking, lighter by two or three pounds. As for the boy, furtive, bright, that's George, too, as he was at Wesley's age, a few months either way. It's a Wednesday, carefully selected (Mom meeting Dad in city, shopping before, pot roast with carrots and potatoes left in a low oven, a check-in promised but maybe not; they trust him; he is, after all, a sober little citizen, with *opinions*, more likely to be locked in his room listening to *Coward Sings Himself* than Springsteen or Van Halen). It's just before noon; the boy has walked out of school, calm, colorless, like a man in a crowd who knows he's about to commit a crime, which in his case is to flee the country, even for a couple of hours, and come home with a secret, any secret, although he knows that the list of areas he'd like that secret to be taken from grows shorter, and more thrilling, by the hour, producing in him a scent cut and balanced by the scent of fear. As for the list, sex *is* the list; what else would it be? George sniffs for himself, for the scent that stops when the secrets of your life die off, like a species, when you no longer properly protect them because they don't matter anymore.

As the train starts they look out the window to see, through the snow, a series of billboards for *A Chorus Line*; the top hats, the spangles, the strivers with all their hopelessness and gleaming canes. George folds his *Times* using the commuter's origami, as his father taught him to do. The George-boy watches; he is desperate to be taught things by men, rather than to intuit, on his own, what should be hidden from them; hasn't been; will be, soon enough; will be today, in fact, but he doesn't know that yet. *Go!* George said to Kenny. *Oh, but I can't*, Kenny told him. *You know I can't*. George knows this, though. It's the teen on the train; *Go back to him*. This is where he'll be able to keep his promise.

"George?" Something has scared Wesley. Not George's hand on

his arm, or what will happen to him, or where, in the next hour, he'll go. He doesn't know what it is, but suspects it might, again, have something to do with having a wordless adult in front of him, even as he can see George won't be wordless for long. And maybe that's it. Or not. "I don't need to know," Wesley says. "But, I do really want to go in—"

Ah, well; too late. Wesley, without knowing it, is with George in the sudden tunnel that the train enters twenty-six minutes after the trip has begun. He is with him as he comes out into the air and walks, nobly, to the theater district, right where they are now.

"I was fifteen, almost sixteen." Wesley thinks, *Well, that's my age.* But George doesn't; if there's an overview to be had, he doesn't have it; he has nothing but the steps, syncopated, marching into the day itself. "It was matinee day. And what I'd do is get a half-price seat to something, anything, it didn't matter. Then, on this one day—" The famous storm sends him forth, now as it did then, with the three birthday twenties in his pocket from the theater-loving great-aunt, twisted with arthritis, the one he could tell the truth to if he could ever tell the truth. He crosses Forty-second, heads up Seventh Avenue, slowed by the snow and ice and sure this secret journey will yield nothing, that he'll have to turn around and go back, to the pot roast in the low oven, to *Coward Sings Himself.* But that's not how it was. *"It happens,"* George says.

"What does?"

He laughs, as if all Wesley needs is a little reminding, as if he's told him about this day dozens of times when, of course, he's never told anyone about it; no one; not even, since that day, himself. "I finally get into—*A Chorus Line.*"

"What is that?"

"A show."

"Oh, God!" Wesley says. "Is this why I'm up here? To hear about *show business*? And *shows*? I *hate* shows!" George loosens his grip, yet Wesley remains in place. He's cold, and hungry, he hurts in the places he was smashed, and kicked; but even so he knows he is being honored, in being answered, that this man who he insists owes him nothing is giving him something, moment by moment; this gift.

"I walked up at the last minute, and everyone had gone into all the theaters. So the street was empty, for a second. And then I saw this tiny old man, under the marquee."

"You mean like he was a hobbit, or something?" Wesley says; it is his turn now to think, *I wish I hadn't said that.* But maybe it doesn't matter; George, clearly, doesn't seem to have even heard it; he never gets Wesley's references, as Wesley never gets his.

"And it's the last possible minute. Everyone else has gone inside. The doors are closing and the ushers are saying, 'Curtain time.' And the tiny man reaches into his pocket and pulls out a *ticket*, which he holds in the air."

"And that's how you knew you were gay." Again he wonders, *Why did I say that?* And again, perhaps luckily, George doesn't seem to have even heard.

"It was for standing room. The ushers were closing the doors. I offered him some money but he shook his head; he wouldn't take it. He presses the ticket in my hand and points me to the last open door." George isn't aware, although Wesley might be, that he has moved from the past tense into the present.

"So you go in."

"And it's begun. There they all are, holding their pictures in front of their faces. And there's this guy." He stops, not because this is a reliable tale and he knows where the pauses go, but because small lost *sections* of the boy beside him, a bit older, probably, but not much, offer themselves to be sorted, arranged, made into an image. Winter coats, gloves, scarves on the ledge where they both rest their arms. "He's standing next to me. Around my age; he'd probably ditched school that day just like I did. The show starts, I'm loving it, then I notice something."

"Really? What?" Wesley whispers these questions, as if trying somehow not to wrest George out of this moment from twenty-five years ago.

"This guy's sort of looking at me. So I look at him. And then he whispers, 'Are you gay?' And at first I don't understand him. He says it again: 'Are you gay?' And I say, 'Yes.' And I also say, 'Thank you.'"

"You remember that?"

"I seem to," George says. "I *think* I do."

Then, for a moment, the crisped pictures, predigital, in the album fade. George questions them all; the tiny man, the open door, the crimson ledge on which they rested their arms. *I haven't thought of this since then, or felt like this,* George thinks. This is the revival of a moment, like a play brought back years later, with a different cast. What has time changed? It's not that time heals everything, George knows; it heals what's convenient, what's easy to heal. Someone once said that to George, someone before Kenny, long ago. Time can afford to be lazy because it has nothing but time. Well, George doesn't. He has only now.

"Can *I* ask a question about that?" Wesley says.

"Of course."

"Why do you think you said 'Thank you' to that guy?"

"I don't know," George tells him. "I don't think I've ever

thought about it. Maybe because it made it real? Or made *me* real, anyway."

"Well, that's a thing to say thank you for."

"You think?"

"Definitely. So is it all right for me to tell Theo that?"

"Sure," George says. "If it helps."

The night shifts a little, and sighs, gently trotting in a dream like a dog in its bed.

"And you got home," Wesley says, "and told a lie. Because you'd never say what had *really* happened, or where you'd *really* been." He laughs. "Not that I'm judging it! Because I lie, too, sometimes, which you shouldn't know, probably. Not because I'm such a liar, although I am, but more as this kind of moral/existential/epistemological test, in a way. Which I know is a lot of tests, but the question of what is truth is a fairly large one, one might say! Me and Theo feel, personally—this is the kind of stuff we talk about—that lying is most interesting as an *action* when you don't actually have the *need* to lie. Does that make any sense? Because it allows you to find out what truth, personally, is for *you*. Because there have to be more categories, quite frankly, than *truth* or *untruth*. Which is to say: *lies*. Theo says everyone needs to choose their own cherry tree. By which I refer to truth, not fruit. Or he does. Not that you asked." He pounds his palm against his forehead. "I even bore myself. How can you listen to me? Promise me you'll never like secretly record me, okay?"

"I can't do that, Wes."

"Why not?"

"Because I don't know what's going to happen."

"No," says Wesley. "Right. You don't." Someone across the street, on the fourth floor, opens a window. His tv volume is up high. *"Hello, Jerry,"* they hear. Then *"Hello, Newman,"* which Wesley recites with the tv; he and Ben love *Seinfeld*, and have seen every episode. Then, just as fast, the set is turned off.

"Can I ask one final, *final* question?" Wesley says. "Which you totally do *not* have to answer?"

"Sure. Why not?"

"Before I asked you and before up here—had you thought about it like that?"

George doesn't answer. He peers out over the building's edge, into the small, on-the-grid, wrapped box of streets; this theater district that can never again be what it was and yet is still full of swirling dollars, bouncing tunes, mobs of the satisfied-enough and the vindictively, revengefully disappointed, on their way home to anonymously leave, on screens, the *opinions* the screens so greedily demand. Up here, though, they are far from all that. George sees things that he hasn't seen before, and wants to point them out to Wesley. But Wesley, he remembers, knows this rooftop well; he hasn't been afraid to come here.

"I believe you," Wesley says, seeing in what George has told him how it is possible to have an experience and only find out later what it means; that part of the nature of experience is how it insists on the right to keep parts of its meaning a little bit secret, revealing the balance when the time is right. "It makes you wonder," Wesley says, "about what else might be up here, on the roof, I mean. Does that make any sense? I don't mean the *literal* roof; I mean the roof as a *notion*. As a place where things live, one might say; things that neither of us know, that could maybe even be *answers* to things. Who knows, I guess. Right?"

"Right."

"So I'm the first person to ever hear that? You never told it to anyone before?"

"No."

"Why," he says, not putting it as a question, wanting information more than an answer.

George knows what he would like to say, which is the first thing that comes to him: *Because no one ever asked.* But that's not it, quite, and not fair; nowhere close to what Wesley would call the *thing.* So, once more, George lets that join them—the thing itself—and hosts it as he might at Ecco, this George who can be relied on to be welcoming and insignificant at once. So, then: Why? Because when he came to the city, at eighteen, it was a time when the young men and those a little (but not much) older were less interested in tales of when they knew than in rich, fibrous knowing itself, all that you had to be up on in order to keep up at all; the lore, the facts, what Lenny called the admission price to Gay Street. And so George, when he says to Wesley, "I don't know," is telling the boy the truth.

Wesley knows it. "I believe you," he says; he wants to stress that, too. "Really. And you should hear the Theo fable, or saga, or whatever it is. It takes place at our school, which isn't exactly known for psychosexual-revelation incidents. There's this bird, see, and a ball, and *Citizen Kane* is in there, too. Don't ask."

Don't ask; an expression George uses daily. Lenny (again) says you need a little Yiddish if you want to survive in New York (and who wouldn't?); he is convinced that Jackie Kennedy, among friends, referred to her second marriage as that whole *mishegoss* with that bug-eyed Greek *momzer. Don't ask.* George wonders: *Did he get this from me?* And yet, Wesley doesn't follow his own shrug-shouldered, rag-trade advice. He asks all the time; he asks, and asks;

and answers are, after all, what they're doing up here. "I won't ask," George says. "Don't worry."

"But can I ask something?"

"Oy," says George, not hoping for a laugh, and not getting one.

Wesley doesn't wait for George to give permission. "What you just told me," he says. "Have you ever told that to my father?"

His *father*; George has never heard Wesley refer to Kenny as anything but *my dad. Maybe that's what happens up here,* he thinks. He sees a penny on the roof; how did it get there? He decides that he must pick it up, now, or something terrible will happen to them both. He takes a step or so toward Wesley, circles behind him, kneels for the penny, and puts it in his pocket. Now he sits on the ledge where, moments ago, Wesley was *Boy, Reading*, turned away; *I just want to be alone up here.*

"George—"

George shakes his head.

"But you told me," says Wesley.

Did he? He doesn't even know. "I guess."

"No. You did. So, don't guess. Not to be rude."

"If you say so," George tells him. "And you're not, so you shouldn't worry about that." He feels separated into parts; retinas, arteries, discs all laid out on the roof, the pieces puzzled as to how to come back together as: *him.* As whoever he is, or was.

"Which must mean you trust me, sort of. That is, I guess. In a way."

"I do."

"You're the first, then," Wesley says. "The first real person, I mean, by which I suppose I mean *adult.* Well, you know what I mean."

"I do," George says again.

"Thank you."

"I don't think I'll be the last." He is suddenly aware of life at windows; all the books being read (which would please Lola), profiles scanned, downloading, uploading, links being sent; *I thought you'd like this.* . . . He hears the sigh of the man who has just masturbated to the porn site (*This is the last time*), the clink of tags as dogs join couples on beds, lights going out and couples turning to or away from each other.

"So you're *sure* it's okay for me to tell that to Theo?"

"That's up to you."

"Then I won't," says Wesley. "Your secret is safe with me, if that's what you want."

"I know." He reaches into his pocket, finds the penny, passes it to the boy; who takes it, says nothing, puts it in his own *ciambelline*-crumbed pocket. "So where does that put me in your Hall of Guys?"

"What?" He looks puzzled, as if he'd never heard of anything like this.

"Like Obvious Guy, remember? Or what was one of the others . . . Literal-Minded Guy?"

"Oh." Wesley is neutral.

"So I know who I'd be. Recollecting Gay Guy. How's that?"

Wesley is careful now, with each word, as if giving instructions to a partially deaf babysitter. "You're not in the Hall of Guys," he says, "at all. Sorry."

"Ah," George says, familiar with the evoked response: *One more team that doesn't want me.* "Of course. *Too gay!* I get it."

"*No*, George. You're not in it because you don't need to be. Because you're just *you.*"

"That's a good thing?"

But Wesley's moved on. "Do you want to know where I was?"

Wesley knows he does, so he doesn't have to wait for the assent. "Among other things I went to see Theo," he says, "who's fucked up."

"What do they say?"

Wesley doesn't answer this. "And I went to Ben and Mom's. I didn't see her; I will. She was making salmon."

"So she uses the poacher?" George asks him. "That's good. Most people don't use the poachers you give them."

Wesley doesn't answer this, either. "It just sort of made sense, after I went for this walk with Ben, to come here next." They share a picture, at the same moment, without knowing it; of Wesley's night flight; a toy plane flying over a map, tracing its journey in dotted lines, as in what George thinks of as a good movie and Wesley thinks of as an old one. "Ben *cherishes* her, George."

"I can see that. I always have. They're lucky, both of them."

But Wesley shakes his head, as if George hasn't understood him. "*Cherishes* her." He has netted the verb and traps it, humming, in his hand. "That was his word. I know what it means, but I'd never heard it in that way before, one person using it about another, as this sort of significant *verb*. And I asked him if that was better than love."

"What did he say?"

"He said I'd find out. That he was sure of it. So what do you think?"

"I think you will, too. I'm sure of it, like Ben."

"You don't understand, George," Wesley says. "I'm not talking about me; I'm tired of me." He puts up a hand, to forestall George's support. "Which doesn't mean you have to, like, bolster my self-esteem. I'm constantly bolstered; it's sort of insulting, actually, like people think without the bolstering I wouldn't have any at all. Not that you do that. I don't mean you."

George indicates coldness, as a bad actor would, with hunched shoulders, big shivers, arms wrapping around himself. "It's getting cold. I'm freezing my ass off up here."

"No, you're not," says Wesley.

"Well, it's my ass, right? I should know."

But Wesley has no time for this. "So what do you think? Is it better than love?"

"Oh, my God," George says. "Why would you ask me that? *I* don't know." He feels like he does in a dream, the great, reliable dream of forever, the one he still has even years after acting was through for him; where he is waiting in the wings to make an entrance in a play, realizing at the moment he receives what he knows to be his cue that not only hasn't he learned his part, but he was never told what his part was. He is on his own; he could be anyone; and no one.

But Wesley doesn't know about the dream. Again: he needs an answer. "But maybe I do," George says. "If it helps. I *do* think so. Yes." He says it again, stronger now, to lock it down because he knows it, suddenly, to be true. *"Yes."*

"I don't know why I know this," Wesley says, "but I bet they'll always be together." He nods at his own observation, like someone at a rally agreeing with a point in a speech. "Maybe I'm wrong, but I just sort of know that."

"You're not wrong."

"Really?"

"With some couples, you just know. Right?"

"Oh, right," says Wesley. "Totally." He's thrilled, again, without quite knowing that's what the sensation is; *an adult has agreed with his insight into adult life*; he has been given a permission slip to *see.* And that signed paper has, scrawled on the back, the next question he needs to ask.

Which is this: "So, what about you?" George's face, with its slight, sudden, frosted look of panic, gives him *more* permission: *Hang in; do not retreat, no matter what he says; stay.*

"What about me?" George asks, although, of course, he knows.

"Maybe I should be more specific," says Wesley. "In the interests of clarity, which I know is a thing I say a lot. But—" He looks at George; he sees that he has him, that for this moment George will not look away. *Just ask.* "You and Dad."

"Ah."

"Do you cherish each other?"

George doesn't answer; not because he won't; he can't. He is too busy seeing the roof's sudden show of the hundred reasons, laid out like exhibits at a trial, for which he admires Kenny: the medallions, the certificates, the bits of engraved Lucite; the sheaf of op-ed pieces, the statements carefully crafted. And the things he likes: the cleft chin, the taut-enough stomach, the sculptor's hand. And the sister, the Alice, whom George has just learned of after ten years together; up here now, too, along with the outhouse man, asking if Kenny can come again and Kenny saying they're leaving tomorrow. *No. I was right, downstairs, when I said it. We don't know each other; we never have. Knowing is the father of cherishing. It is where it begins, and ends, too. To allow that is the gift. And it has not, in this time, been given.*

"George?" Wesley isn't waiting for an answer; he's seen what the next question needs to be. "Does Dad cherish you?"

The patch of roof, for a moment, on which they have come closer and closer together, contains two different kinds of silence. George smiles; his face has always known what to do that is best for the moment, for the beat; the scene. But the smile quickly fades, as if ashamed of itself, and as it does George feels he is no longer on a tar-papered rooftop but on a polished square of floor, a *Swing Time* floor, in the process of seamlessly breaking from the brownstone beneath it, like icing lifted from a cupcake. He doesn't dare answer Wesley's question, or even move; if he does, a crack might open and he will fall through, headlong, not just four floors down but into all the rivers of this island the Dutch gave up in a day and wouldn't fight for, not when faced with the stronger, better-dressed, more amusing Britons.

"Is it okay for me to ask you that?"

"It's okay," George says. "I think so, anyway."

Wesley doesn't wait for more; he now gives permission to himself. "Do you think you'll be like Ben and Mom?"

"That people will just know, you mean."

Wesley gently directs George's eye to the clear, even readable words. "That you're one of those couples—"

George takes over. "Who'll always be together. Right?"

Wesley nods.

"Well," says George; he laughs at himself for never having thought of this. "I don't know."

"Okay," says Wesley.

"But thank you," George tells him again, without quite knowing why.

"What would happen to you?"

"What happens to anyone?" George asks, and catches himself, instantly apologizes. "Sorry. What a bullshit thing to say." He spins it in the direction of Dietrich, in *Touch of Evil*; world-weary, wig askew, secret lover to the great and attractively infamous. "Vhat happens to anyvun?"

But Wesley, happily, is a clueless audience. "Where would you go?"

"Oh, you know," George says, even though *he* doesn't. *Does anyone?* he thinks. Well, yes; many do; there are armies of lucky people to whom fatalistic philosophies don't apply. George has even been one of them, for a long time. Or thought he was; which is the same, until things change and you have to choose, in the night, the three things to put in your suitcase.

"Actually," says Wesley, "I don't."

Now George is not, especially, a queeny queen, but he does know, he realizes, the imaginary cities where one can go to be tragic, whispered-about, a veiled *condesa* with a backward daughter. "Zurich first, probably."

"Are you serious?"

"Oh, yes. *Ja.* I miss Germany."

"I don't mean this to be literal-minded, or anything, or rude?" says Wesley. "But Zurich is in Switzerland, more or less."

"Well, of course it is."

"So, where would you go?"

All right, then; here it is, or here *he* is. George, who has never been one to fear the future or even, much, to consider it; for him it has been nothing more than the next place, that then gives way to the place after that; none of those places, surely, to be feared. Nor does he fear death, and never has; what Lenny refers to as the Table for One, in off the street with an hour to kill, no reservations, might as well be here. If anyone were ever to ask George why he doesn't fear the things most people do, he would see, perhaps, that yes; it has to have been the road; it was where he formed his just-the-next-place philosophy, on buses smelling of French fries, old gum, sleeping people who know they will never rise higher than this; buses bearing him to two nights here, three there; the next places much the same as the places before; the same scrappy museum, rich lady's garden, the same depressed downtown. Next places; never new ones. And, then, death. *He died the death of a salesman.* George was Biff, twice, so he knows the play; he has always understood what Willy meant. You do your job, and then it's done, while you were still in the act of doing it. You've gone nowhere, maybe, but you've kept your hands busy; you have not risked being still, because to do that would be to open yourself to questions, from others and, maybe worse, yourself.

So as for now? There's this building, its claws dug into the flesh of the street; below them, the tight fourth-floor rooms, and the subterranean bit of Tuscany; he has been here for ten years, believed he had loved here, kept it stocked with bread, flowers, stories in which he's the comic lead; dear George, clueless, silly, slow to see. But he sees, now, that this has never been more than a place between places, the stop longer than most. Has he always known this? "I don't know," he says at last.

"Well, that sucks."

"You think?"

"I mean not to know," Wesley says. "That's all."

They both start to notice how cold it is and act it out for each other, shivering and shrugging, synchronized, like a dance team.

"Hey, George?" Wesley says, even though they are looking right at each other.

"Yeah?"

"I don't know why I feel the need to tell you this, exactly? But I'm not gay, actually. Well, I don't mean *actually*? But you know what I mean. Right?"

"Now, *that's* something I do know," George says. "At last. Something!"

"Or I don't think so, anyway."

"Well, things can change."

"They can?"

George bites his lip; he wants the joy of telling Wesley something ridiculous, to fool him for a moment (this kid will believe anything) and then, deliciously, resolve his worry. "Well," he says, "one day you could be walking down Sixth Avenue, right? Which is where things like this usually take place, somehow."

Wesley, he sees, is already a little worried. "Like what kind of things?"

"Transformations, of the Gay Kind."

"That can happen?"

"There you are, and all of a sudden there's thunder and an eclipse and this Great Gay Rain starts to fall. And everyone suddenly has very white teeth and eight percent body fat and they're all singing 'Being Alive.'"

Wesley stops him. "What is 'Being Alive'? Is it like a song?"

George laughs. "Yes," he says. "But all you need to do is *be* alive. Don't worry about *being* it."

"Good," Wesley says. "About not needing to know, I mean. So at least I can be consistent, because I don't know anything."

"Well," says George, "as has been well established, neither do I."

Wesley looks out, over to Ninth Avenue, as if Ninth Avenue held the answer to the question he's privately asking himself: *Does anybody know anything?* "Nobody does," he says, still looking out. "It would seem. Do they."

"No."

"Do they," he says again, and again without a question mark; for he knows the answer, himself. "I should tell Theo that. We missed our Fact today. I should tell him it's a fact that nobody knows anything. Other than facts, I guess. Right?"

"It would seem that way," says George. "Yes." And facts, now, are everything; George can nearly see them, waving their hands and insisting they be called on. *He loves this boy*; he sees and acknowledges that. *He could be kept from seeing him again*; he can see that, too; possession, or nameability, is not only nine-tenths of the law; it is the law. And then the fact that doesn't insist, because it doesn't have to; it is the one George has always known, in one way or another, in situations other than this. *He would like to give something of value; he has nothing of value to give.*

"But I know something," Wesley says. "It's just one thing, but I know it's true, and I'm sure of it. Is it okay if I say it?"

"Please," says George.

"It's just that whatever I become? Whoever I turn into—" He looks down; his fingers brush the slightly raised caterpillar of stitches above his left eye as if they were a Braille that might tell him what to say next. Then he nods, just once, as if he's come to a final agreement with himself. He looks up, his eye now on a direct route to George's. "I know that I want to be like you."

George laughs; or maybe the laugh steps forth, before he can do or say anything else. Words come forth, as well—*I don't think you mean that*—that sound like they're coming from somewhere else, from another rooftop.

"But I *do*," says Wesley. "I want to be like you."

"Oh," George says now; all other words have left him; it is all he can think of to say.

"So would that be okay? Because I completely mean it."

"I know you do," says George; and he does. "But why would you ever want that?"

"I just do. I can't *explain* these things, exactly."

"No, no, of course you can't." He says this, maybe a little too quickly, wise and seasoned about an exchange he's never experienced before; he realizes that Wesley's words have scared him, have demanded something he doubts he can give, which is a clear-eyed story of himself. So, in a voice that seems to echo back to him, as if the night sky above was no more than the high ceiling of a dark blue room, he says, "But what do you mean? What *am* I like? In what way would you want to be like me?"

"Well," Wesley says, "in the interests of clarity, I don't mean I want to be like this big fag, or anything." George laughs, out loud; he can't help it. "Not that I'm insinuating that you're all that big?"

"You can say it. I *am* a pretty big one. In fact, I'm—"

Wesley puts up a hand, to stop him. "Don't. Don't say a funny thing."

This has been like water, sprayed at an unruly puppy; George is stunned, at first, then shakes it off. "Sorry."

"I want to be how you *are.*"

"And tell me how that is," George says, now, forgetting all he knows of himself, giving it up, releasing it, ready to learn from this boy. "How am I, Wes?"

"Don't you know?" Wesley says, gently. "You're *there*, George."

"There," George says. "Okay." Wesley's gaze has not freed his; he feels rubbery, leaking gravity like motor oil; were he to lightly jump on the roof he would not be surprised to find that it was, actually, a trampoline, with all New York as its net, that would bounce him up high for the sport of it, with no promise to bring him back.

"That probably doesn't make sense. I know I *don't* make sense, mostly, and you don't have to say I do, because I see your lips starting to form supportive words and phrases. I *know* you, George." He takes the penny George found from his pocket, blows on it, polishes it on his sweatshirt; he holds out the penny to George. As a gift; without a word.

George takes it. "There," he says, echoing Wesley's word for him.

"Which you are," says Wesley. "Which you've been, George. For me."

There; just that, alone. Where they are now, in fact, in the fixed center of the night, a brief safe place while the borough bubbles and aspires below them. And from this new place George can see that, while this boy has been with them, he has for the first time seen himself as a full man, and complete; this has nothing to do with defeating a belief that Men Like That (his preferred term) cannot, by their nature, ever be complete men; he doesn't believe it, for one thing, about himself or others. No; it has more to do with the sense of himself Wesley has, just by being there, provided. How can this have happened? He is nothing like the boy George was; a matinee liar, a secret traveler on morning trains. But, somehow, he has taught George words to the spell to summon that boy, to give him a rooftop on which to speak the hundred secrets he was so sure he could never tell, secrets that, over time, he has even learned to keep from himself. George knows now that the boy he has heard above him, on the roof, working out his steps at 2:00 A.M., is *that* boy; himself, he has always been waiting. And to see him again—awkward, lumpy, *undelightful*—is to see at the same time a glimpse of the richer life he would like to lead and has been afraid to ask for. He can't yet isolate the elements of that vision. But he has help now; there are two of him; together, they are a place from which to start. So where do they go?

"Hey, George?" Wesley says suddenly. "Look!" He points to a window in the building across the street; a young man stands there, waving. "That guy!"

George looks. "Oh, him," he says. "That's just Eddie. He's in *Wicked*; he comes in sometimes, after the show." He waves back, calls out. "Hey—!"

"George!"

"Yes?"

"You can be so embarrassing!"

"Thank you," George says. It is delicious, he finds, to mortify a teenager, even if the witness to Wesley's eternal shame is just one *arrabiata*-loving Flying Monkey; he even makes a little bow. "So I don't know about you, but I'm freezing my ass off up here."

"You've said that."

"Well, this time, it's true."

"Not to be rude, or anything."

"I didn't take it as rude, or anything," says George, not mocking him. "So maybe I'll go in. Would that be good?"

"Go in?" Wesley says, puzzled. "Why?"

"You said you wanted to be alone."

"I did?"

"When I came up. You don't remember?"

Wesley, for what seems, to George, in his vivid, dream-like fatigue, like an endless elastic moment, doesn't answer. Then, at last, he does. "Well, maybe you should go in," he says. "Because you're probably really tired. I know you hear me up here, and not just the other night, or whenever it was. All the nights. Sorry. You need your sleep."

"I *don't*," George ridiculously says. "So don't apologize. I was up, anyway."

"Of course you need your sleep! It takes energy to be like—"

"What?" George says, wondering if Wesley has one more adjective to offer.

But he doesn't. George can tell. He looks down, shuts his eyes, just perceptibly moves his lips as if telling a story to himself. At last, he looks up.

"Hey, George?"

"Yeah?"

"Can I maybe ask you a question?"

Questions, answers; it's how they began. *Is your name by any chance George?*

"Of course you can, Wes," he says, throwing in at the last moment the second syllable, "—ley."

But he shakes his head. "No," he says. "Forget it."

"You sure?" He nods. "So I will go in, then," George says.

Wesley doesn't stop him. George turns back to head for the little door. As he stoops to go through it, he hears "Hey, George?"

He turns. "Yeah?"

"Does my dad love me, George?"

"Oh, my," says George when he hears this. "Oh, my."

"That wasn't fair," Wesley says. "I shouldn't have asked you that."

And here is what George does, after he notices how close Wesley has come to him, close enough to touch. And he does touch him, this son of others; without thinking or seeing himself do it he puts a hand on his shoulder. "You did ask, though," George says. "And he does." Does he know that, as a fact? No. But he believes it, is even sure of it.

"Okay, then. Thank you."

Another nearby window opens. Someone is watching tv; George hears a few notes of music and knows it is Bernard Herrmann's score for *Anna and the King of Siam.*

"And you're right," Wesley says.

"About your dad?"

"The cold! I'm freezing my ass off up here, too." He steps back, to shake off the weight of George's hand.

But George won't let go. "No," he says.

"But I have to go."

George grips tighter. "Where?"

"Somewhere," Wesley says, flushing, panicked as a person might be trying to get the attention of an unheeding crowd after an accident has occurred. "Please, George."

But George doesn't let go. "You're forgetting something," he says.

"I am?"

"You had another question."

"It doesn't matter," says Wesley. "Whatever it was."

"You asked me, yesterday, or whenever, if I felt it was a choice. *It.* Do you remember?" Wesley nods. "And I never told you. I never got to say."

"You asked if you could think about it," Wesley says; a boy who respects thought, who puts it near or at the top of the list of human activity. "So?" He shifts his shoulders, so George's hand can more easily rest there; he does not want to break away. "George?"

But he sees right away that he doesn't have to say that. George is there, even before the calling of his name, before Wesley can finish saying it. "No," he says; he waits to see if there are words behind that, waiting to join them on the roof. There are, but they are organizing themselves, calling up the courage to be heard, and seen, their gazes cast down as Wesley's, sometimes, significantly is. "No," says George.

Wesley's hand shoots up, on its own, like someone who knows the answer before the question has been fully asked. "You mean like Dad said, when I asked you guys," he says. "Like when he said how could it be, because—"

"No," George says, to stop him, and Kenny's words, too. "I don't mean that at all." He says this because he knows, suddenly, that it's not like that for him, not as it seems to be for Kenny, who always knows so *easily*. George doesn't, and even when he does he struggles to see it and, even harder, to express it. For no one has ever asked him to express anything; he is not the man for that; you go to George, lovely, impeccable George, for *recommendations*, knowing he will steer you to an endless calendar of agreeable evenings. But it's different up here; that has just changed. "I don't even know what I want to say here," he says. But, right away, he sees that he does know, and he can't keep this a secret from Wesley. "But that's wrong. Because I do." He starts to take his hand from Wesley's shoulder, but Wesley steps forward and angles slightly to keep it there: *Not yet. Stay close.*

"I'm here," says Wesley.

George starts slowly, like someone who has been in a hospital bed for a long time, has come to know its deliciousness, and also knows this is the day he must leave it, that his return must begin *now.* "When a person says that of course it's not a choice, because who would ever choose it—"

"A person like Dad, you mean."

"Oh, no," George says, much in the way he said, *Oh, my, oh, my.* And, for a moment, that's all he has. As he looks to Wesley and sees him nod, he realizes he's been squinting, as if to blur any hovering visions of Kenny, or anyone; even of a self he thinks he knows. "No," he says, once more. "There are people who *would* choose it, you see. I want to be clear about that."

He never talks like this. Wesley knows that, as he will never forget, at least for a while, anyway, the sight of a man becoming *willing*, in front of him, to be someone other than who he's been. "You're being clear, George."

"Good. Because there are a lot—" He's lost now, for a moment, and he's never lost. But he's also never ventured out this far. Wesley, sensing this, puts *his* hand now to George's shoulder, to steer him home, to show him how close to home he really is.

"You were about to say," Wesley says, "something about a lot of—"

"Yes," says George. "There are a lot of people in the world who would choose it."

Wesley laughs.

"What?"

"You're shouting a little," he says. "Actually, in the interests of clarity, a lot." He is not embarrassed; he is fascinated, and impressed, at how George seems to be *addressing* the street, the theater district, the city itself. And George laughs, too; at his nascent noisiness and, also, because he no longer feels perilously hoisted; the roof, with its outward view, starts to settle, becoming a safe place for him to stand.

"I'm sorry," George says.

"Don't be!"

"Good. Because I'm really not."

Now George laughs, tickled by how he's quickly killed his lie, before it could sink its teeth into him. He steps back from Wesley's touch, looks around and sees, suddenly, how much room there is up here; he starts to take long, diagonal surveyor's strides, slightly bent in Johnny Appleseed fashion (a role he played in the fourth grade), pondering the soil beneath him. When he comes to the center, he stops, straightens up, fills his lungs with the crisping November air. He looks up, to the stars, the local set that he and Lenny have always believed are unique to the theater district, with bright promises of Laurette Taylor in *The Glass Menagerie;* the Lunts in *The Visit*; Gertrude Lawrence in *Lady in the Dark*; the lost great things, all of them returned, with good seats available always.

George looks down now. "And what I was going to tell you—about choosing—is that *I* would choose it." He looks up. "*I* would choose my life. All right? Are you listening?" Wesley nods; George sees something he's missed, that Wesley has come closer; he is close enough to touch. And he does touch him; the boy is gravity for him now. He thinks, *I need him, just for a moment more. Just one.* "Because—when you *step* into your life . . ." He laughs at himself; for having put it like that; at his fresh dream of life as a series of houses, entered through doors that have been waiting to open, without keys. "And you're *in* your life," he says, "I mean, truly *in* it . . . I just hope—"

He stops, perilously, like a wind-up toy at the edge of a coffee table. Wesley worries; he wants and needs more. "George?"

"Yes," George says, and to stay standing, as the ground beneath him shifts, he places his other hand on Wesley's other shoulder, each arm now a bridge. "I just hope you feel about your life how I feel about mine. Do you understand that?"

Wesley nods; he does, and he feels understanding, sweet and prickly, flow through him. "I do," he says. "You cherish it."

"That's right. Whatever happens. I do. So if you still want to be like me?" Wesley nods. "Then be like me in that."

"I will. I'll try."

"Do that."

"So I guess we should go in?" Wesley says.

"Oh, I guess," says George.

But they don't go in; they both look up, as if they'd received the same text at the same moment, telling them to watch as a thin, curling cloud completes its glide across the moon, followed by another, and a few more, still, that the sky seems to supply from nowhere.

"It's awesome, you know," Wesley says, using the word his mother so dislikes.

"What is? The sky?"

Wesley laughs. "A *day*. A lot can happen in a day, I mean. If that makes any sense."

"It does." The thin, curved moon, like the wandering element of an emoticon, is clear again. "That's what days are for."

They each look down now, although not yet at each other. Cabs, whistles, bullets; buses, screams, small sobs; people singing, sighing, pleading with dogs to shit; from the long streets the *clang* of texters bumping into lampposts; the soft fall onto the ground, like leaves, of seven thousand flyers bearing news of who was out for tonight's performance; the audible thoughts of select citizens, taxpayers, permanent residents: *Today I worked; I loved; I tried.* All of it, some louder, some softer, but never less than *all of it*; so many sounds to take in that the boy and man, having just agreed on the capacity of a day, don't hear the next one, which blends in, which is the man from just below, having come up the steps to find them, clearing his throat as he steps through the door onto the broad roof. They hear him, finally, as he coughs a second time. As they turn to him, he nods, and then raises his hand to wave, to his son and his love, as if to make sure they see him.

The End

ACKNOWLEDGMENTS

Marshall Herskovitz and Edward Zwick gave me a true gift on the shows I was lucky enough to work on with them (*thirtysomething; My So-Called Life; Once and Again).* They had one note for me, pretty much always: *Be more you.* This note is as uncommon in television as it is in life. Hearing that for several decades helped me see that my own passions, worries, hopes and mistakes—my life, in short—made a worthy subject. They said that what you write should have the intimacy of a letter to a small circle of friends, people to whom you never have to apologize, or explain yourself. So *These Things Happen* is a letter to them; the old fashioned kind, with a stamp. I'd like to send that letter to others from those experiences, as well. Liberty Godshall, Susan Shilliday, Scott Winant, Winnie Holzman, Ken Olin, Peter Horton, Melanie Mayron, Patricia Wettig: check your mailboxes. And thank you.

My parents, Claire and Allan Kramer, have always encouraged me, enjoyed me, and given me enough room to be always, sometimes perplexingly, myself. Books, reading, words; they loved all these, and saw that I loved them, too. When I am in my 90's, as they are, I hope to have some portion of their openness to experience, their deep sense of responsibility, and their endless and surprising forgiveness.

My editor, Greg Michalson, hung in there with me while, during my improvements on the book, I nearly destroyed it. He snatched it from the fire I had unwittingly built, and taught me, after years of being a writer, what it means to be an author.

In 1976, fresh out of college, I had a job as an assistant at G.P. Putnam's. The girl at the desk next to mine talked faster than anyone I'd ever heard and thought faster, too. When I was nearing the end of writing this book I asked a Knowledgeable Someone who he thought was the best literary agent in New York. "Gail Hochman," he said. Could she be the Gail of long ago? Was Hochman her last name? I e-mailed her; she got back to me instantly. Of course she remembered me! I should send the book. She called the next day, ready to take *These Things Happen* under her steady and able wing. She never gave up, or gave in; her passion never wavered. "I've never been wrong when I love something," she said. That love found a home for the book, and the right one. I am forever grateful to her.